"You can lie to me, but not to yourself, Ms. Butler," Andre said smoothly, as he took a step closer to her

"You want me right now just as much as I want you. But you should know that I will not confuse this attraction with my obligation to protect my family."

Joanna stepped back and squared her shoulders. He obviously knew what buttons to push, because he was right—she did want him, though she'd never admit it. "Your conceit knows no boundaries, does it?"

"Don't you want me?" he teased. He licked his lips seductively. Joanna didn't respond, but Andre had his eyes focused on the lusciousness of her full coral lips. Their slight quiver gave him all the answer he needed. Without thinking, he reached out, grabbed Joanna by her waist, pulled her body close to his and kissed her.

At first she was too stunned to move. Her lips were already parted, so Andre took full advantage and inserted his tongue. His strong arms encircled her and she grabbed on to him desperately, relishing every moment.

Books by Celeste O. Norfleet

Kimani Romance

Sultry Storm

Kimani Arabesque

Love Is for Keeps
Love After All
Following Love
When Love Calls

CELESTE O. NORFLEET

is a native Philadelphian, and has always been artistic. But now her artistic imagination flows through the computer keys instead of a paint brush. She is a prolific writer for Kimani Arabesque and Kimani Romance as well as Kimani TRU, the young adult line. Her romance novels, realistic with a touch of humor, depict strong sexy characters with unpredictable plots and exciting story lines. With an impressive backlist, she continues to win rave reviews and critical praise for her spicy, sexy romances that scintillate as well as entertain. Celeste lives in Virginia with her husband and two teens. You can contact her at conorfleet@aol.com or P.O. Box 7346, Woodbridge, Virginia 22195-7346. And don't forget to check out her Web site at www.celesteonorfleet.com.

When It
Feels So
Right

CELESTE O.
NORFLEET

KIMANI™
ROMANCE

To Fate & Fortune

KIMANI PRESS™

ISBN-13: 978-0-373-86131-6

Recycling programs
for this product may
not exist in your area.

WHEN IT FEELS SO RIGHT

Copyright © 2009 by Celeste O. Norfleet

www.kimanipress.com

Printed in U.S.A.

Dear Reader,

Each time I sit down to write I think about the characters I want to create. Then I begin with a simple idea and let my imagination go from there. This time my imagination really soared. I've always been fascinated by Alaska and its tumultuous beginning. This story gave me the opportunity to explore that idea.

That said, I'm thrilled to bring you a new family, the Buchanans of Alaska—sexy, rugged men and strong, sensuous women.

Jo Butler and Andre Buchanan are the perfect pair. Their story is passionate, soulful and hot enough to melt the ice caps. Surrounded by a kaleidoscope of great characters, I know they'll win your heart as they've won mine. So sit back and enjoy! If you want to hear more from the Buchanan family let me know and I'll be happy to comply. Until next time.

Blessings & Peace,

Celeste O. Norfleet

ACKNOWLEDGMENTS

Special thanks to Paulette Jones, Lorraine Morris Cole and Dorothy "Aunt Dot" Andrews. Thanks also to the readers who keep me grounded and focused on getting it right. I'd also like to thank in no particular order: Louise Brown, Roben Rasheed Hernandez, Sharon Clark, Jennifer Johnson, Sharon McCalop, Bobbie Austin, Eleanor Shields, DaKia Scott, Tiffany Wilkerson, Kaia Alderson, Beverly Jackson and the ladies of LiveLaughLoveandBooks.

Chapter 1

"Come on, come on, where are you," Joanna Butler muttered to herself as she turned and scanned the area for the umpteenth time. Crowded, then not crowded in alternating waves, the tiny Juneau airport had gotten crowded again. She stood in a walkway with her baggage all around her. People could get around her easily enough and she had no intention of moving one inch. She sighed heavily. She was tired, hungry and impatient. She had already spent almost an hour waiting for a man who obviously had no concept of time.

"Jo, if he's not there by now I think you should just turn around and come back," Pamela Gibson, her best friend and agent, said over the phone.

"No, I can't, I gave my word I'd finish this," she answered.

"Excuse me, you're blocking the entrance," a man's voice spoke from behind her. Without interrupting her phone conversation she stepped aside. "Other way," the voice instructed. Slightly annoyed, she turned and looked up. Tall, dark and gorgeous smiled down at her with an amused expression on his face. His voice was deep and rich and his smile was generous as his soft brown eyes sparkled.

"Good Lord," she muttered way too loudly, as her breath escaped her and her heart thumped solidly in her chest. She was greeted with a smile so sexy it weakened her knees.

He appeared to be about six feet three or so, with a rich, milk chocolate complexion. His jaw was slightly chiseled and perfectly complemented his high cheekbones and teasing single dimple. He was clean shaven with a hint of hair just below his lower lip. She watched his lips move. He said something but she had no idea what it was. His mouth was the best part, full and sensual. He sent instant, unexpected shivers through her body.

"Jo, is that him?" Pamela asked through the receiver.

"Hold on a minute, Pam," Jo said.

"Excuse me," he repeated coolly, with a slight smirk of enjoyment on his full lips. He was obviously amused by her expression and reaction. She shook her head but still didn't respond. "You're blocking the path," he said, pointing to the corridor behind her.

She turned around, then back to him. "Oh sure, of course, sorry," Jo said, pushing her luggage out of the way and blindly stepping backward. She was accidentally bumped by a rushing passerby and nearly tumbled forward. A split second later strong firm hands grabbed, held and steadied her. Pressed intimately close to what felt like heaven, Jo didn't protest since the speeding airport cart nearly clipped her leg. Seconds later she was released and she instantly felt her body object. Not paying attention, she had almost walked right into the cart's path. "Thanks," she said breathlessly.

"Anytime," he said, "are you okay?" She nodded then leaned back against him again. "Are you sure?" he asked, holding her securely once more.

"Yes, I'm sure, just a little shaken. Thank you." She looked up at him again and smiled. Suddenly he looked so familiar. "I know this sounds like a pick up line, but do we know each other?" she asked.

"No, I don't think so," he said, obviously amused.

"It's just that you look familiar." She shook her head. "Never mind, well, I guess I owe you for saving me."

"I guess you do," he said smiling.

"Joanna," she said, removing her glove and offering her hand to shake his.

"Nice to meet you Joanna, my friends call me Cannon."

"Cannon," she repeated, "that's an interesting name."

"Perhaps I'll tell you about its origin some time."

The seductive way he spoke left little to the imagination. They had definitely connected and the instant strong attraction between them was escalating. "I'd like that."

He nodded. "Are you here on business or pleasure?"

"Business, and you?" she asked.

"Business, but there's always time for a little pleasure."

"My sentiments exactly," she said smiling, enjoying his assertive directness and easygoing charm. "Are all Alaskan men as charming as you?"

"Sure," he joked, "it's in the water."

She laughed. "I'm waiting for a ride and it looks like I might have been stood up. Can I buy you a drink or coffee? It's the least I can do for the man who saved my life."

He looked around briefly. "Can I get a rain check?"

She nodded her understanding. "Sure, another time. Thanks again for saving me," she said, wanting to say more, but for some reason couldn't. He nodded and turned to leave.

She decided to take a chance. "Wait." A few feet away he stopped and turned back to her. "Here, for the rain check." She handed him her business card then watched as he proceeded down the corridor. A sly smile touched her lips.

When he held her she caught the scent of his clean, fresh aftershave. Now she inhaled deeply, savoring the last remnants of possibility. She couldn't remember the last time a man held her close, let alone made love to her with his eyes. She sighed. That's all she'd be getting for the next few weeks. She was on an assignment and that meant complete focus on the task at hand. But there was no harm in one last look. With as much discretion as humanly possible, she did exactly that.

Tall, dark and gorgeous, how do you not stare? He was dressed in straight leg jeans and an open neck white shirt with a sport coat, and he moved quickly and purposefully. Mesmerized, Jo watched his long, even strides and his tight rear walk away. It had been a long time since any man sent instant quivers down her spine and this man sent them in abundance. Forgetting for a moment that she was here on business, she considered the possibilities, then shook her head and bit at her lower lip. *Have mercy.*

Yep, this is what men were supposed to look like, she told herself with a broad satisfied smile. Then completely unexpectedly, he stopped and turned, looking directly at her. She nearly crumbled with embarrassment. It was as if he'd heard her lustful thoughts. He smiled again before turning and going about his business. "Way to go Jo," she muttered to herself, "way to charm the locals."

"Jo, Jo, are you still there? Is everything okay, was that him, did you find him?" Pamela asked.

The insistent chatter from the other end of her cell phone grabbed her attention. She'd forgotten all about the conversation she was having with her friend. "Yeah, yeah,

I'm here. No, I didn't find him yet, but I just figured out why I can't find a man in New Jersey, they're all here."

"What?"

"Nothing, never mind. I'm still waiting."

"Still no sign of him, huh?"

"No," Joanna said, watching the corridor just in case tall, dark and gorgeous returned. "No sign of him yet."

"I guess at this point trying to talk you out of this craziness is a complete waste of my time."

"You can't talk me out of it and this isn't craziness. I need this and you know it. If I don't do it now, I never will."

"Granted, you need a break after everything you've been through the last few months, but this is a bit on the drastic side, don't you think? You've gone from one extreme to the other."

"Not at all. I needed a change and this is it, and if I remember correctly, it was your idea originally."

"As a joke, Jo, as a joke. I was trying to lighten your mood after all the drama. Who would have thought you'd take me seriously? You never take me seriously."

"Well this time I did and it was a good idea. Please thank your mom again for passing it on to me. You know I need this both financially and emotionally. I can't spend another day in New Jersey. I just hope this works out and I can finally finish it this time."

"It will and you will. You're a great ghost writer, Jo. You'll do justice to Jacob Buchanan's biography. He's lucky to have you, even if you do have to go to God's country, U.S.A., to meet him."

"Alaska isn't the wilderness you think, Pam. Juneau is a nice-sized place. As a matter of fact, the actual area of Juneau is almost as large as Rhode Island and Delaware put together."

"I see you're back in full research mode," Pamela said.

"Yeah, I still have a ton of information from before, and more recently Jacob has been sending me his notes to work on. It's really taking shape. I'm already more than half done. This is the final part, the face to face. Writing Jacob Buchanan's biography is an incredible opportunity. The only obstacle I see now is the rest of the Buchanan family. Getting their input would be perfect, but Jacob warned me that they weren't exactly thrilled about any of this when he told them."

"Of course not. Being that rich for so long, they probably have a million skeletons in their closet."

"I don't know about skeletons, but they have an unbelievable history. I read up on Jacob's oldest son, Daniel, the CEO of Titan. He's looking to run for public office. I think he's going to be the most difficult."

"You're right about that, but a word of warning, Daniel's son is even more dangerous. Andre Buchanan is very good at what he does."

"And so am I," Jo said confidently.

"Still, be careful. If you're lucky you'll be in and out before he even knows you're there."

"I can't wait to meet Jacob and get started again."

"That's *if* the two of you ever meet. Why don't I call my mother again? She's got his private number. Maybe she can get through to him. After all, he's her friend and client."

"Pam, I have his private number, but he's not answering. The phone's turned off. I already left messages on his voice mail. I do have his home address. If all else fails I'll just grab a cab and go over there."

"It's strange that he's not there waiting for you."

"Well, in his defense, I am three and half hours late, thanks to a two-hour delay and a missed connection. I did call him and tell him I'd be another hour."

"So he should at least be on his way there, right?"

"I don't know since I was able to get an earlier flight, so now I'm actually an hour earlier than I assumed when I called him last time."

"This is so confusing. But the bottom line is that you're left standing, waiting in a strange airport. That's not cool. Do you have any idea how unsafe that is?"

"I know, but it's okay. There's a crowd of people around most times." Jo looked around cautiously. After once being robbed at knifepoint, then later having her apartment burglarized and ransacked, she knew what fear was and she wasn't taking any chances.

"Still, you've been waiting awhile," Pamela said.

"Yeah, but we both know this is a big deal. I could use the cash infusion—not to mention it would seriously help my reputation."

"All right, I can't argue with that. But right now I don't know what to think. I can't imagine what happened. I called two days ago and everything was all set. Maybe he changed his mind. You know this hasn't exactly been done before."

"He seemed to be on the level when we started the preliminaries again. I'll wait awhile longer then catch a cab and go to the house and see what I can find out. If anything's strange I'll just grab the next flight out. Either way, I'll call you tomorrow. It must be close to midnight on the east coast."

"No, don't worry about it. Call me tonight."

"Okay, talk to you later," Jo said, then closed her cell and looked around again. Ever watchful, she steadied her gaze on any possible match. No one resembling the man she'd come to meet stood out. There was no way she would have missed a seventy-five year old man with white hair and a white beard.

A quick chill shivered through her. Just like the weather

outside, she was cold, damp and borderline miserable. Warm-blooded by nature, the slightest chill often gave her the sniffles. The next few weeks in Juneau were definitely going to be a challenge. She sighed wearily and bundled her coat tighter. It had been a long tiresome flight and a long trying day that started way too early. All she really wanted now was to sit and relax, but the steady flow of travelers only added to her frustration.

This was her first trip to Alaska. So far the only thing she had seen was Juneau International Airport. It was a typical midsized airport with shops, restaurants, newspaper stands and souvenir kiosks. The crowd thickened and thinned as flights arrived and departed, and still she waited. Everyone was coming and going except her. Impatient by nature, she tried to compose herself as she continually scanned the area. She hated when things didn't go as planned.

This was supposed to be a quick in and out, no fuss, no muss, a few in-depth interviews and that was it. Now it looked as if that wouldn't be happening.

Aggravation furrowed her usual even expression, pinching her perfectly arched brows together. She'd called six times since arriving and had gotten no answer. "Come on," she muttered to herself. "It can't be this hard to find one man." But it was, and the one man wasn't just any man. It was Jacob Buchanan, president and chairman emeritus of Titan Energy Corporation, the largest African-American-owned oil and energy company in the United States.

Titan was a company that few knew much about. It was only lately that it had come to media prominence, prompted mainly by a string of recent family scandals. But the company's beginning was what fascinated her. There was nothing on record. No strike-it-rich oil well and no sudden gush of wealth. It was just there—with a history as mysterious as the wilderness in which it prospered.

As per their many advisories, one thing was definitely known about Titan; they played by their own rules. Rumored to have gained millions by unscrupulous business practices years earlier, they supposedly built a mega-corporation on the backs of honest working men and women. They were said to be ruthless to those they deemed a threat. They were unforgiving and unapologetic. They took what they wanted and did as they pleased.

Unsubstantiated, their corporate value had been reported at more than twenty billion dollars. They belonged to a consortium, and operated just under the radar of the powerful conglomerates. But their profits flourished immeasurably, as noted by their PR person who, of course, claimed that all rumored accusations were unmitigated falsehoods and the result of tabloid journalism and vengeful failed business associates.

Well, this was the opportunity to prove it one way or another, making her a catalyst for the truth. She intended to dig out whatever secrets the family hid in closets, get all the facts and leave no stone unturned and, as usual, remain unbiased and professional. That's if she ever started.

Jo waited another twenty minutes than gathered her luggage and walked to the exit. She grabbed the first cab in sight. She gave the cabbie the address and he looked at her strangely. "Is there a problem?" she asked.

"Douglas Island, this the right address, you sure?" he asked, looking at her in the rearview mirror.

"Yes," she said pointedly. He nodded, pulled the meter flag down and pulled away from the curb.

Chapter 2

Andre Buchanan chuckled to himself as he walked away. He seldom made impulsive decisions like that, but in this case he afforded himself the latitude. His observation skills had always served him well. He'd watched her a few seconds before interrupting. Her body language and posture showed reserved tension. She was stressed and disturbed about something. She frowned as she looked around and spoke on the cell phone. He focused on her mouth. The soft coral tint and moistened luster made him wonder about tasting her.

She wasn't the usual type that attracted him. His tastes ran along the lines of nondescript executives too busy to demand anything more than he was willing to offer. Whereas they were brash and aggressive, she seemed to be the exact opposite. Still, there was something fascinating about her. Sure, he could have walked around her, but interrupting her phone conversation was more entertaining. He intended to disrupt her just long enough to get her attention. But to his delight her reaction upon seeing him made him smile almost as much as her appearance.

Tourists outfitted in what mainlanders presumed Alaskans wore always made him smile. It was late September and the temperature was a moderate thirty to forty degrees, yet she had on a heavy hooded jacket with fur-lined collar, a knit sweater and wool pants. She was layered to the extreme and he assessed the possibility of peeling each layer from her body. Speculation on what he'd find made him smile again.

He knew instantly that she was new to the area. He certainly would have seen her before. A woman like that you don't forget easily. She stood out, even as she tried not to. With a knit hat pulled down nearly covering her face, it took him a second glance to get a better look at her. Light-colored eyes, silky smooth milk chocolate skin, high cheekbones with just a touch of innocent bewilderment. Yet it was her lips that ultimately drew his attention. They were full, sensual and kissable, just as he liked them.

He chuckled again. She stood out, literally, in the center of the airport walkway. That alone he found intriguing. Why would a woman stand in the center of an airport walkway? The psychology of her position could mean almost anything. He knew he wanted to make contact, he just didn't expect it to be so hands-on.

Still, pulling her away from the oncoming cart gave him the opportunity to hold her close for a few seconds. Her expression was priceless. His smile softened then firmed. To his surprise his body instantly reacted to their closeness. That was unexpected.

Afterward, he knew she'd be watching him. He didn't need his doctorate degree in psychology to tell him that. He knew the effect he had on women and God knows he loved reaping the benefits. At six foot three his height and athletic build made him an imposing figure. He enjoyed it. It tilted the balance in his favor. He enjoyed that too.

If he had more time he'd further investigate her arrival in his hometown, but that would have to wait. That's not what he needed to focus on at the moment.

Andre continued down the corridor and headed to the private lounge in the back of the airport bar. He walked in and looked around. Frequented mainly by first-class travelers and persons of notoriety, it was completely secluded. Most didn't even know the small room existed. Unfortunately, his grandfather did.

He walked over to the small narrow bar. A familiar face greeted him with a knowing nod then a quick glance across the room. Andre waited as the bartender poured two cups of hot coffee and slid them across the narrow counter. He nodded, picked up the two cups and replaced them with a hundred dollar bill. He walked in the direction the bartender had glanced. He found his grandfather sitting at a window seat with a young woman by his side. She wore too much makeup, with a top too low and a skirt too high. She turned, looked up at Andre and smiled.

"We have company," she said seductively.

Ever since his grandmother, Olivia, died almost two years ago, it seemed his grandfather had been on a mission to find peace and comfort. The problem was he never could. He was troubled and angry with himself over his wife's sudden death. No amount of anonymous female companionship could ease his troubles, although he kept trying and every gold-digging, wannabe sugar mama readily assisted.

"Excuse us," Andre said impatiently.

"Give us a moment, dear," Jacob Buchanan said, patting the woman's bare leg affectionately. She licked her lips then whispered something into Jacob's ear making sure her ample breasts brushed his arm. "I don't think he's into that," Jacob said. She poked out her full red lips, stood up, grabbed her jacket and sashayed over to the bar. Jacob turned and stared out at the Juneau city lights.

"Hello, Granddad."

Jacob smiled broadly. "Andre, I would ask what on earth you are doing here, but since you seem to always have a sixth sense about these things, I won't bother."

"I'm looking for you," Andre said, placing the cups of coffee on the small table. "Rumor had it you've been hanging around here for the past few hours."

"Why didn't you call? You usually do."

"I tried," he said smoothly, "but your cell phone's turned off again, so I thought I'd stop by in person." He held his hand out. Jacob reached into his pocket and gave him his cell phone while shaking his head and finishing his drink. He grimaced then smiled as the amber liquid burned his throat and heated his insides.

"Don't think I'll ever get the hang of that silly thing, too many unnecessary buttons. I always push the red one too long when ending a call. Blasted thing turns itself off every time." He watched as his grandson turned the phone back on and held it out to him. He took it and placed it back in his jacket pocket. "I thought you were still in New York and Los Angeles putting out publicity fires for Quinton and Cole."

"I've been away for nearly six weeks. I took care of it," Andre said easily.

Jacob chuckled and affectionately slapped his grandson on the back assuredly. "Of course you did. I knew you'd handle it with your usually clever manipulation. Who better to send into a media snake pit than a snake charmer?"

"Not exactly, but close enough," Andre said, knowing

that his grandfather's remark was more true than not. As Director of Public Relations and Communications of Titan Energy, his job was to maintain the public perception that highlighted the company's vast advances while negating its many public transgressions. Thanks to his brother Quinton and cousin Cole, his job had become increasingly more tedious. He had to quash bad PR on a daily basis.

His latest public relations nightmare was Cole's ex-girlfriend who, along with her attorney, decided she deserved a percentage of his Titan stock by way of a paternity suit. She'd gone for public sentiment by playing the destitute ex versus the rich businessman. While the Titan and Buchanan lawyers did their part, he did his. By the time the paternity test came back negative, her reputation as a con-woman was revealed as well as several other previously undisclosed lawsuits. His ex wisely withdrew the suit, citing unspecific reasons.

More recently he wrapped up his brother's case, which had been slightly more complicated. Quinton had been sued for sexual harassment by a former employee. The case was nearly airtight and the media was all over Titan personnel. The end result was that the complainant was found mentally unstable with fixation issues. They'd settled out of court to cut their losses and sponsored her full treatment. In both cases Cole and Quinton had been completely exonerated, but Andre was still fighting public opinion since the damage to their reputations had already been done. But that was his job.

Now on his way back home for a few days of rest and relaxation, he got a call about his grandfather sitting in the airport lounge for hours. He had to come.

Still, he hadn't had a moment to himself in weeks. His nerves were frayed and his frustration level was through the roof. Perhaps that was why the last "problem" didn't exactly turn out as he planned. He cleared his cousin of course, but there were adverse repercussions that he still had to deal with.

"What was your strategic battle plan this time?"

"No plan, I just relayed the facts."

"Overwhelmingly to Quinton's and Coles's advantage, of course," Jacob prompted.

"Of course," Andre said, tipping the corner of his full lips slightly. Anyone watching might not have noticed a difference, but it was there. It was the slight smirk that relayed his restrained pleasure. "So what time is your flight?"

"My flight?" Jacob asked.

"Yes, I spoke with Dad earlier and he mentioned that you and he are meeting to discuss the consortium proposal in Anchorage tomorrow morning."

"No, we canceled. That's next week."

"I was told that you canceled last week, and rescheduled it for tomorrow."

Jacob paused a moment to consider his schedule. "Ah yes, so I did, so I did. Well, that's unfortunate."

"Why is it unfortunate?" Andre asked.

"I'm here waiting for a very important appointment," he said.

"So I've heard."

Jacob raised his brow with interest, "I know you haven't been siccing your countless spies on me, have you?"

"I don't have countless spies, Granddad, you know that," he replied with cool efficiency without actually answering the question. It was his usual tactic and it seemed to work well. "So who exactly are you expecting?"

"A friend," he said evasively.

Andre looked around. "Anyone I know?"

"No."

"What's the name?"

"Jo."

"Joe what?" Andre asked.

"Jo Butler."

"I don't remember you ever mentioning a friend named Joe Butler. Is he a business associate?"

"Hardly and more or less," Jacob said, chuckling to himself.

Andre smiled and shook his head. The evasive game his grandfather often played usually meant that he was about to do something the family wouldn't approve of. The last time was with the interior designer he hired to redecorate his bedroom.

She in turn seduced him then claimed that he was the father of her unborn child. It was later discovered that she was already a few weeks pregnant when she arrived in Juneau and that she'd dangerously slipped him several performance enhancement pills causing him to be rushed to the local hospital. Needless to say, when the family learned what she'd done they sought swift and severe retribution. It was Jacob who resisted and instead offered to set up a college fund for her child. Embarrassed, she declined his offer. With that disaster avoided, Andre kept a particularly close eye on his grandfather's actions.

It wasn't that his grandfather was old and senile, it was that Jacob Buchanan had a huge heart. He gave more and trusted more than he should. Since his retirement from the company, he became more and more reclusive and more and more trusting. Plus, he enjoyed occasional female attention. It came out later that he knew exactly what the designer had planned. Either way, Andre wasn't about to have that happen again.

"Actually, Jo's more of a friend of a daughter of a friend. You remember Lydia Gibson, she owns the professional fund-raising and concierge agency I use from time to time. The one that…"

"Yes, I remember Lydia's Lifestyle Management Agency quite well," Andre said, knowing that he wasn't going to like what followed. The last time his grandfather and Lydia put their heads together he had to bail his grandfather out of jail and elaborate an outlandish story to appease the shareholders. Fortunately the media bought it as just another Titan publicity stunt to raise awareness for global human rights. Andre glanced around, looking for a slightly overweight redhead with a laugh that would scare a witch. "Granddad…"

"Now don't *granddad* me. I'm not in my dotage. I know you and Lydia have butted heads a few times over the years. She's a good friend and a damn good business-woman. I've never requested anything that she couldn't provide."

Andre sighed. This was exactly what he feared. His grandfather's requests had a tendency to wind up on the front page of some tabloid newspaper. "Exactly what have you requested this time?"

Jacob looked beyond Andre. "Ah that must be Jo," Jacob said, smiling as a young woman entered the private lounge and stared at them as she approached. He stood. Andre turned and stood, following his grandfather's lead.

The woman approached, nodded, then continued past their table. She turned to smile at Andre as he looked at his grandfather, realizing his mistake. A cold chill sliced through him. "I take it that wasn't Joe," he said as both men sat. "Also, I presume this Joe is a woman."

Jacob smiled, "Indeed she is." Andre closed his eyes and shook his head. This Jo was exactly what the family didn't need right now. Jacob instantly took exception. "Now don't give me any of your 'time to save Granddad from himself' guff, I know exactly what I'm doing. Jo will be staying with me for as long as it takes. We have things to do."

"If you needed a secretary, Granddad, why not…"

"A secretary, Andre? If I needed a secretary I'd simply relocate one from corporate headquarters in Anchorage. No, this job is far more specialized."

"Specialized? Granddad, please, I must caution…"

"Don't go cautioning me, Andre," he warned firmly, "this is nonnegotiable. Jo will stay with me at the cabin." He stood to make his point, but wobbled slightly instead.

Andre instantly stood and grabbed hold of his grandfather's arm, steadying him. He looked around and nodded to the bartender who immediately picked up a phone behind the bar and made a call. "Granddad, what I mean is that maybe this isn't the best time to invite a stranger into the Buchanan circle. With Dad preparing to run for a senate seat and our plans with the energy commission, perhaps we can…"

"Nonsense," he said firmly, "this is the perfect time. We'll be fine. Your father's political ambitions can only benefit from this. He'll be vetted by the party anyway, why not let our truth be told the right way, our way. We'll eliminate all assumptions and falsehoods."

"That's not exactly how it works, Granddad. The truth has little to do with historical fact. Man has a way of making his own truth in history, recording it as his ego dictates."

"Including the Buchanans, and that's exactly why Jo's coming," he said, chuckling. Then seeing the stern seriousness of his grandson's expression, he reached up and patted his shoulder. "Oh, no worries, Andre, time has been kind. The Buchanan family secrets are buried deep enough that even I can't find them anymore. Just as well I'm sure."

"Eventually time runs out and secrets are never quite buried deep enough in some regards," Andre mused. He noted his grandfather's assistant, Bane, had entered the lounge.

Jacob nodded. "I've been assured that Jo is an excellent writer and she…"

"A writer," Andre interrupted, "this Jo is a writer."

"Of course, how else am I going to have my memoir written? I needed to hire a professional biographer. She comes highly recommended with an excellent professional resume. Even you, dear grandson, won't be able to find fault with her."

"Granddad, we talked about this months ago. You said you were going to hold up on that until later."

"I don't know if you've noticed, my boy, but I don't have too many laters left. At seventy-five I feel the urgency to tell my story my way. Now."

Andre backed off knowing his grandfather's resolve. "Fine, I'll handle it. I'll find an adequate biographer, one more sympathetic to the family history. It'll take a few months, but we'll…"

"Not necessary, Jo called earlier. She missed a few connections and her flight's a bit late, but I'm sure she'll be here in no time."

"And what about the energy commission meeting?" Andre asked. "As chairman emeritus and founder, your presence is crucial."

"Ah yes, that is a bit of a pickle. Perhaps we can postpone it until next week."

"No, Granddad, the meeting has already been postponed twice, once for Dad and once for you. Another postponement might make the commission overly cautious. This new venture is a Buchanan lead after all. We don't want them to have second thoughts."

"No, of course not," Jacob said, seeing his assistant at the door waiting for him. "I suppose I'd better attend."

"Excellent, I'll wait here, meet your Jo and send her away until this is settled," Andre said, knowing of course that he intended to pay Jo off to leave permanently. "There is no sense in having a stranger staying at the house unsupervised."

"No, of course not, that's why you'll have to stay and continue the job without me. A good part of it has already been written and sent to her. I've also dug out some family information. I want this completed as soon as possible."

"Me, work with your writer? No, Granddad, that's not possible. I'm too busy."

"Of course it is. The two of you working together can get it done in no time. You can start tomorrow. I'll join you in a few days."

"No, that's impossible. If you'll remember I'm attending the commission meeting as well."

"I'll make your apologies," he said firmly. "This is far more important."

"Far more important than changing the direction of the company?" he asked. "More important than expanding our company and possibly altering the energy direction of the country and quite possibly the world?"

Jacob chuckled easily. "See, now that's why you have the position you have. Your verbal skills are unmatched. You could talk the devil into central air conditioning. But it won't work on me, not this time. My mind is made up and I think it's an excellent solution," Jacob said. "This way, Jo can get started, I'll have my memoir working in my absence and you'll be directly supervising the progress."

"Granddad, I'll tell you what, let's just get you back to the cabin, I'll wait for your writer and we can talk about it when I get there—if, of course, this writer of yours arrives."

"She'll arrive, you make sure of it," Jacob insisted.

"Fine," Andre conceded. Jacob nodded as he allowed Andre and his assistant to walk him through the terminal to his waiting car. Andre kept a steady pace showing no cause for concern or alarm. One thing that can be said for the Buchanans, they rose to every occasion publicly. They never showed weakness because appearance was everything. Always loyal and always family first, it's how they were raised, it's how they lived. In the public eye and under the media microscope, they each made sacrifices for the good of the company and the family. It was just expected.

Clearly he didn't need this right now, he was stressed enough. After just arriving home from litigation in New York and before that handling the media frenzy in Los Angeles, he didn't need this. He stood watching as his grandfather's chauffeur and assistant got him in the sleek black town car and drove away. Thankfully the whole scene was kept low-key. The last thing he needed was to have the newspapers find out the patriarch of the Titan Energy Corporation was hanging out in the airport lounge waiting for a woman named Jo.

Andre turned and went back into the airport knowing that if he wrote a check large enough, this Jo would certainly turn around and head right back to wherever she came from. He stopped by the information desk and requested a page for Jo Butler every fifteen minutes for the next two hours. Afterward he decided to spare a few minutes looking around for Juneau's newest arrival. Perhaps he'd take some time to get to know her before this next Buchanan implosion.

Chapter 3

They'd long since left the bright lights of Mendenhall Valley and were now headed toward downtown Juneau. Jo looked out the window to see what local sights she could see in the murky darkness. She knew that Juneau was tucked between the mountainous terrain on one side and a narrow body of water on the other, but seeing either was impossible. Adding to the darkness and lateness of the hour, visibility was decreased because a heavy saturating mist had settled over the area.

The cab continued traveling in complete darkness along Egan Drive. It had been only fifteen minutes, but it seemed a lot longer. Along with the mist came patches of an ice-cold drizzle. It fell like a curtain and for a time she focused on the cab's wiper blades as they pushed the frozen rain aside.

It had gotten colder outside. She shivered and gathered her heavyweight jacket closer around her neck. What was she thinking? Obviously late summer in Alaska wasn't exactly late summer everywhere else. In actuality, it was more like winter in her hometown of Florida. But she could take it. She could take anything at this point. After all, she was in Alaska about to complete the perfect assignment.

Every biographer she knew would give their right arm to be in her place. She eased back, closed her eyes and considered her upcoming assignment. The jovial voice of Jacob Buchanan came to mind. They'd had several phone conversations. He'd been the perfect gentleman, charming, attentive and charismatic. How could she possibly turn him down when he suggested she continue the interviews and research immediately? She smiled just thinking of him. But she cautioned herself not to grow too attached to her client. She made that mistake the last time and it was a disaster.

Detached and remote, facts only, she reminded herself. *Don't get personally involved.* Although she'd found Jacob charming and congenial she knew that a man like him had to have more skeletons in his closet than the local cemetery. Since the project originally started two years ago, she needed to refresh what she knew about her client.

Jacob, son of Louis Buchanan, was a billionaire businessman recently retired after the death of his wife. He became chairman emeritus of Titan, leaving running the company to his son and family. Although his father, Louis, started the company, it was Jacob's insight that took it in a new direction and made it one of the most successful small oil companies in the world. She reviewed several more facts then took a deep breath. Taking on this job was guaranteed to be nerve-wracking, but she looked forward to it.

Still chilly, she quieted her chattering teeth and drifted

off calmly, peacefully to a place between sleep and consciousness. She rested comfortably for a while until troubled half dreams intruded, centered on past drama and strife. Then feeling the cab's slight jarring bump, she jumped and opened her eyes. The bridge was ahead. She knew she was close. "Do you know of a ferry that crosses here?" she asked.

"This time of night, other than the bridge, swimming's the only other way to get to Douglas Island, lady. The ferry's closed for the night," he said, adding a gruff chuckle at the end.

"Thanks," Jo replied tartly, noting his sarcasm. She tried to relax against the backseat again, but found it impossible. She was too excited. She closed her eyes thinking about the last few months. She'd gone through hell and back, her reputation had been trashed and her career was teetering on the edge of an abyss. She needed this time away, but most of all she needed this job.

Eventually she felt the cab's slight bump then back to the steadiness. She opened her eyes just as the cab cleared the bridge. Just as she relaxed her cell rang. "Hello?"

"Hello, my dear," Jacob said in a welcoming tone. The genuine softness in his voice set her at ease instantly. Old enough to be her grandfather, at least, she found that she'd been looking forward to hearing his voice.

"Hi, Jacob, I'm in a cab, I'm on my way to your house now."

"Oh, well, that's good to hear. I think I missed you at the airport, damn crowded terminals."

"That's okay, are you still there?" she asked, looking around at the darkness again.

"No, I'm on my way home as well, but my grandson is I'll call him and let him know that you've already arrived."

"Your grandson?"

"Yes, Andre, I believe I mentioned him to you, didn't I?"

"No, I don't think so," Jo said, without adding more. It had been two years and her outdated research had been primarily centered on Jacob and his father, but she still remembered Andre Buchanan. He was a man few women could forget. As soon as she reconfirmed the assignment, the first thing she did was to gather and review her old notes and reacquaint herself with current information on Jacob and the immediate family.

It hit her, the man at the airport, minus the beard of two years ago. "It was him," she said aloud.

"Excuse me," Jacob said of her odd remark.

"Oh, nothing, just thinking out loud," she said. "I promise to be on my best behavior. Your grandson will adore me."

"That's exactly what I wanted to hear," Jacob said.

She looked out of the cab's side window. "Jacob, my cab just crossed the bridge onto Douglas Island."

"Excellent, you should be there shortly. I'll phone ahead to have the gates open. I'm certainly looking forward to finally meeting you."

"Me, too, I'll see you soon," she said, then closed her cell and smiled. Just the brief conversation was all she needed to ease her frayed nerves. And of course there was Andre.

Since the job had ended so suddenly and she wasn't exactly up on oil and energy now, she hadn't heard about or seen Andre Buchanan in two years. No wonder she didn't recognize him without his beard. She smiled, remembering a few not-so-chaste fantasies she had had about him at the time. "Good Lord," she muttered.

The cab driver looked up in the rearview mirror, "What's that?" he asked.

"Nothing," she said, slightly embarrassed by her thoughts.

It had been two years since she'd seen a photo of him. In that time she hadn't thought about him or any of the Buchanans since the job ended midway through. They didn't know each other, they didn't travel in the same social circles and she had no reason after all this time to even consider him. But if memory served, Andre Buchanan was the most elusive front man she had ever read about. They called him *the charmer*. Supposedly he was so charming, yet evasive, cunning and persuasive, that when he spoke, the media was instantly enamored. He was vice president of PR, but apparently stayed completely out of the limelight himself.

She remembered his academic background and his professional accomplishments, but everything else was, as per the Buchanan family, a complete mystery. She also remembered that he was considered smooth, cagey and would probably be impossible to circumvent when it came to getting information. Thankfully she'd be dealing directly with Jacob. But it wouldn't hurt to loosen up and use her charms on Andre a bit. The more family support she got the better.

Several miles down the road, driving in almost darkness the cab driver finally stopped and shifted to park. He glanced in the rearview mirror at her. "All right, what now?" he huffed.

Jo looked up and saw that they'd stopped in front of a tall iron gate. There was a call box off to the side. "Push the button," she said. He did. Nothing happened. He pushed it again. Again nothing happened.

"Doesn't look like they're expecting you," he said gruffly. She didn't reply. Then without warning a green light shined and the gate unlocked and opened slowly. The cab drove forward down a well-lit path then turned into an open area parking in front of a large structure. She paid and thanked him with a large tip then covered her head with her hood and got out. Seconds later the trunk popped open. Just as she grabbed the handle of a small valise, the cab driver hurried to assist her. "I'll get these up on the porch for you," he said.

He made two trips piling the cases at the front door. Joanna thanked him again as she climbed the steps with her purse and laptop. "Looks like you've got company," the cabbie said, looking behind her down the driveway at the approaching car. Joanna turned around to see a large black car pull up and stop behind the cab. "Have a good one," the cabbie added, as he went back to his car, got in and drove back down the long driveway.

The car's driver quickly got out just as the back door opened on the opposite side. The driver hurried around to hold open the door as an older gentleman got out. He looked up at Jo standing on the porch and smiled. "Jo Butler, I presume." She nodded and smiled. "At last," he said happily.

Jacob, along with his assistant, walked up the steps to meet Jo. He took her offered hand, shook it and then kissed her cheek. "It's a great pleasure to finally meet you face-to-face, my dear. After all of our phone conversations and interviews, I feel like we've known each other for years."

"I feel the same way, Jacob. It's a pleasure to finally meet you in person. I still can't believe I have this opportunity. It's truly an honor to work with you. You're a legend."

Jacob chuckled. "Well, I certainly hope not, at least not yet. Come along, let's get you out of this damp weather. This is Bane, my personal assistant." They greeted each other with a polite nod. Bane opened the front door. Jo turned to retrieve her luggage. "Don't worry about that, Bane will take care of them."

"Thank you," she said, as Bane began gathering her luggage.

"Sure," Bane said, with an easy smile.

"Come in, come in. Let's get you inside and dry. I'm sure you're not used to our weather just yet."

"Actually it is a bit surprising. I wasn't sure what to expect when I looked up the weather for Alaska online. I'm just glad I packed warm clothing."

"This is the rainy season. This time of year Alaskan weather can be unpredictable, cold one day, warm the next. Come, dry yourself by the fire or would you rather freshen up first?"

"Actually, freshening up sounds like a great idea. I've been traveling since early this morning."

"Of course. Bane, please show Ms. Butler to the guest room."

"Sure," Bane said, already loaded down with several pieces of her luggage. He waited on the first landing as Joanna walked to the stairs to follow him.

"When you're done just come back down, we'll have a nice chat before dinner's ready. I hope you're hungry?" he asked.

"Yes, as a matter of fact I'm starved."

"Excellent, a woman with a hearty appetite. I'll meet you back here in the drawing room in, let's say, forty-five minutes?"

"Yes, perfect," she said, following Bane upstairs.

They walked up what could have been considered a grand staircase, had it not been for the complete lack of posh. As with the rest of the house, everything seemed purposely understated. With the money Jacob had, she assumed he lived in the lap of luxury, but instead, his home was more like an oversized cabin in the woods.

"So, Bane," she began, following him down the lengthy hall. "Tell me, is Jacob always so friendly?"

"He's exactly the same as long as I've known him."

"How long have you worked for him?" she queried.

"Not long, a few years or so, give or take," he said.

"So what do you do around here?"

"What don't I do around here?" he joked easily.

"Are you from the area? Alaska, I mean."

"Sometimes it feels like it, although I guess no one is originally from anyplace anymore."

"You're probably right," she said, realizing that he hadn't actually answered any of her questions with a definitive reply.

"This house is beautiful," she said as he stopped at a door and set one piece of luggage down. He opened the door then stepped back to allow her to enter first. Jo walked in and was instantly astonished by its beauty. "Wow, this is for me, are you sure?"

"Positive," Bane said, grabbing the case he had set down then following her inside.

Jo turned and smiled. "Aha, so you can give me a straight answer."

Bane chuckled and looked away slightly embarrassed. "Well, after a while you learn to play cards close to the chest."

"I completely understand. Don't worry, I'm not here to write a scathing exposé, just a facts-only bio. So unless you have a mass of information about Jacob's childhood, I wouldn't worry about me using anything you say."

"Thanks, Ms. Butler."

"Please, call me Jo," she said.

"Thanks, Jo." He proceeded to show her around the guest suite pointing out the bathroom and a sitting room with a huge walk-in closet, and a balcony. There was also a small alcove set up like an office with a desk, chair and bookshelf.

"This is perfect. Thanks, Bane."

"Anytime. I'll get the rest of your luggage up here while you're at dinner. I think I'll check on Jacob now," he said as he walked a few steps and turned back to her. "To answer your question, yes, Jacob's a great man. I've known him all my life. When my mom died my sister and I came to live with my grandmother who worked for his late wife. When my grandmother died Jacob and his wife kind of adopted us into the family, and I've been here ever since. He's a good man."

Jo nodded, touched by his story. "I agree. He is a good man. I'll see you downstairs in a few."

When Bane closed her door Jo walked over to the bed, held her arms out wide and collapsed back. The giddy feeling of being here completely immersed her in calm. She looked up at the vaulted fifteen foot ceiling beyond the large four-poster bed. The room was like a suite at some grand hotel. She could definitely see herself getting used to this. Her condo in New Jersey, as nice and comfortable as it was, didn't even compare.

A few minutes later she opened a suitcase, grabbed a fresh outfit and hurried into the bathroom. Ten minutes later she emerged wearing jeans and a hunter green sweater with simple jewelry and feeling completely refreshed. She checked out the office area again noting anything she might need and then headed downstairs.

As she came down the steps the front door opened. A man entered talking on his cell as a cold wind blew in behind him. She continued down the steps observing him curiously. From behind he looked familiar. Then it hit her, it was the man from the airport, tall, dark and gorgeous. The corner of her mouth curved upward. So this is Andre Buchanan.

* * *

The conversation, which began on the phone shortly after Andre left the airport, lasted for the next fifteen minutes. The two men talked about myriad topics ranging from the current political climate and his chances of unseating the local senator to the end result of his New York and Los Angeles trips. Andre assured his father that as far as he was concerned, everything was under control.

They went on to discuss the meeting the next day and the best way to garner the additional support they needed to keep control of their interest without being swallowed up by the larger companies. The idea of mergers and hostile takeovers wasn't completely foreign. It had been tried many times. For some reason the idea of a prosperous, exclusively African-American-owned oil company was bait for every would-be game hunter in the northern hemisphere.

What these predators didn't know was that Titan Energy had the complete support and backing from three of the largest oil companies in the United States. By mutual consent Titan needed their support and vice versa. Titan, thanks to Louis's and Jacob's connections, was the only company to have sole ownership of lifelong land and offshore drilling permits. They couldn't be touched. If Titan went down it would cause a domino effect on the rest of the companies. As long as their backing remained solid and constant, hostilities were kept at bay. No businessman was so stupid as to challenge all three mega holdings in order to raid them. It was a delicate situation, but one that had worked for decades. But all that would change shortly.

Andre briefed his father on the current situation regarding Jo Butler. "Damn, I thought I'd already taken care of this." Daniel Buchanan said gruffly.

"What do you mean?" Andre asked.

"Dad told me about his plans to write a biography months ago. Then about five weeks ago he informed me that he intended to hire someone. I discouraged it, but apparently not firmly enough."

"Why didn't I know about any of this?"

"I needed you focused on Quinton and Cole. My senate announcement is in a few weeks and I didn't want any family scandals hanging over my head. So, how are you going to end this before it goes too far? What are your plans?" Daniel asked.

"I'm not sure yet, since this is the first I've heard about any of this," Andre responded, as he easily swerved through bridge traffic arriving on Douglas Island. PR troubleshooting was individual in most cases. He couldn't use the same tactics for every situation. Some required subtlety and tact while others needed a more forceful hand. Until he met Jo, he had no idea what direction he'd present.

"Are we sure this Joe Butler is who he says he is?" his father asked.

"The Jo is a woman."

"A woman, are you sure about this?" Daniel asked, obviously agitated.

"I'm positive," Andre said.

"Damn, another woman at the cabin. I knew this was going to happen," Daniel said angrily. "Every bimbo gold digger on the west coast is probably lined up waiting for a shot to strike it rich. We can't afford to have another scandal like last year. That woman damned near cost us a contract with her bogus baby accusations. We don't need this right now."

"I agree. I'm on my way to talk to Granddad now."

"Fine, talk to him, but realize it's a long stretch. You know how he is when he makes up his mind about something. You need to keep *her* away from *him*, not the other way around."

"How do you suppose I do that, baby-sit?"

"Be creative, distract her," Daniel offered.

"Why don't I just offer her money?"

"Fine, try it, but I think you need to be more proactive this time. She may not be a pushover like the others. Perhaps you can run interference. Get between them."

"You're suggesting I seduce her?"

"I'm suggesting you do whatever it takes."

"I haven't used seduction to get a woman for personal gain since college. With rampant sexual harassment charges, it's not worth the risk. But I'll keep my options open," Andre agreed.

"Damn, this couldn't have come at a more inopportune time. We have too much riding on this meeting tomorrow, not to mention everything else we have going on."

"Understood, but Granddad is insistent. Apparently he went to Lydia to get her. I'll contact Ben to begin an extensive background check."

"Good, we need to know everything about her."

"Don't worry, I'm on top of it, Dad. This won't get out of hand." He sped down the dark road leading to the massive iron gates. He pressed a button on his dashboard. The gates opened instantly. He drove up to the house and parked beside his grandfather's black car. Seconds later he bounded up the front steps and opened the front door.

"See that it doesn't. A chopper will be there first thing in the morning to bring Dad to Anchorage. You'll only have a few days to get rid of her. I don't have to tell you that time is of the essence."

A cold wind breezed in as he opened the door. He quickly closed it and continued listening. "Understood. I'll call you and let you know how it's going." Andre said, and then closed the phone. He turned and looked up. The woman standing on the landing stopped.

They looked at each other, but said nothing for a few seconds. "It *was* you," she whispered with a smile.

"You," Andre said softly, as soon as he realized that it was the same woman from the airport. He walked toward the steps just as she came to the last one and stopped. They stood eye to eye, his expression stone cold.

"We've met," she said easily. He nodded once. "At the airport, you grabbed me away from the cart." His eyes narrowed. Her once mildly curious expression was changing to surging confusion.

Amused, he spoke as he extended his hand. "Andre Buchanan. And you are?"

"Joanna Butler, Jo Butler." She extended her hand, remembering what she had promised Jacob. There was no way that he was going to find fault with her. She needed this job and messing up wasn't an option. "It's a pleasure to meet you, Mr. Buchanan," she said.

"So you're the person my grandfather hired."

"I'm the ghost writer, yes." A sudden uneasy nervousness spiked through her.

Andre's expression didn't change. Still assessing her, he shook her hand but held it slightly longer than necessary. He smiled inwardly then walked over and leaned his back against the handrail. He crossed his arms and gazed at her with interest. "So, you've come to expose the family secrets," he challenged.

She stiffened her back defensively as his dark penetrating eyes glared at her. "Excuse me?" she asked, trying not to show how annoyed she was getting.

"Isn't that what you do?" he asked, knowing it would knock her off guard. It was one of his tactics.

"No, I'm a better writer than that," she replied, showing spunk.

Her response intrigued him. He smiled knowingly. "I presume you've already met my grandfather," he said, changing the subject.

"Yes, I have. Jacob is a wonderful man. I think we'll partner well together. I'm excited to continue writing his story."

"I bet you are."

His tone was edged was sarcasm. She picked up on it instantly. "Excuse me?"

"Just making an observation," he said. "My grandfather is indeed a wonderful man. He doesn't deserve to be made a fool of for anyone's personal agenda. And he's not in the market for a permanent partner arrangement, understood?" Jo opened her mouth, but nothing came out. "Am I to interpret the pause as a sign of admission?"

"Admission of what? What exactly is it you think I intend to do here, abscond with the family jewels or the family patriarch?"

"It's been tried before."

She shook her head knowingly. "Oh, I see. I'm the enemy here to topple the mighty Titan Empire with a tawdry tabloid-like bio." He didn't respond. "To put you at ease, I'm just here to do my job. I write what I find and what I'm told and I'm very good at what I do. Your grandfather has my resume and samples. If you're concerned about my credentials, I suggest you check them out."

"I intend to." His pointed reply seemed to end their quick, biting repartee. A few seconds passed with neither speaking.

"Look, perhaps we got off on the wrong foot. I just want to do my job, nothing more, nothing less."

"You should know this whole idea of writing my grandfather's history isn't going to be warmly received."

"So I've noticed."

"I don't like the idea of my grandfather hiring someone I haven't checked out."

"Sounds like something you should take up with him."

"Whoa, whoa, y'all need to chill out and get back to your corners." Both Jo and Andre turned to see Bane walking up. "Hey, Jo," he said easily, and then grasped hands with Andre. "What's up, dude, hey welcome back. Y'all need to keep it down."

"Everything okay here?" Andre asked with added concern.

"Fine, as long as the two of you keep your voices down. I could hear you all the way in the kitchen."

"Sorry, I guess the conversation got a bit overheated," Andre said, looking at Jo's murderous eyes glaring at him.

"Ya think?" Bane said jokingly. Andre smiled and nodded his understanding. It was obvious to Jo they were close.

"Sorry about the disruption," Jo said, "it won't happen again." She looked at Andre knowing that he got her point.

"Well, well, well, here you are. Hello, young people. I don't suppose I've interrupted anything, have I?" Jacob said.

"No, not at all," Jo said, stepping farther away from Andre.

"No, Granddad, we were just discussing your biography."

"A bit more than discussing I'd say," Jacob remarked.

"I checked on dinner. It'll be ready in about twenty minutes," Bane said.

"Excellent, that gives us just enough time for a drink and a bit of conversation in the library," Jacob said.

"Sounds perfect," Jo said.

"Oh have mercy, what a divine creature you are," Jacob added, admiring Jo in her jeans and green sweater. "You look absolutely scrumptious."

"Ditto," Bane said, then heading back to the kitchen.

"Thank you. And thank you again for your very warm welcome. Your home is beautiful and it really is a pleasure to finally meet you. I'm honored to work on your very impressive life story."

"I don't know how impressive it is, but I am ready to get cracking," he said as he slapped his large hands together happily. "I've already dug out several boxes. Bane put them in the office area in your room. My office is down here. It's got a dozen or so more boxes full of documents, receipts, letters and journals. Perhaps we can get started going through them first. We'll need to put them in chronological order and then start…"

"Granddad, perhaps that should wait until later. I'm sure your guest is tired," Andre said.

"On the contrary, I'm fine," Jo said.

"Then after dinner perhaps," Andre suggested, glaring at Jo.

"Ah yes, quite right of course, but first I suggest a welcome drink in the library. Shall we?" Jacob offered, holding his arm out to Joanna. She grasped his arm and was led through the spacious living room to the dining room.

Andre followed. He knew at that moment that he had his work cut out for him. It seemed that his grandfather was already enamored with this writer and he himself had issues that he needed to resolve. Sparring with her was merely a front for what was really going on. He needed her off guard while he regrouped. The problem was that he wanted her from the second he first saw her. His yearnings had only intensified after the clash.

He smiled unwittingly, admiringly. He assessed her a second time that evening. She was attractive, but he already knew that from their brief encounter at the airport earlier. Having changed her clothes, her appearance was more casual this time. He liked what he saw then, and now, seeing the sweet curve of her waist and the abundant swell of her breasts was sending a barrage of signals to his groin. Her hair was down on her shoulders and she looked every bit a seductress. He tensed, feeling his body react again. She was getting to him without even trying.

Earlier, he'd been taken off guard. Understandably he was tense, it had been a long week and the pull of sexual release was exactly what he needed. Long business trips and being consumed by a heavy work load had a tendency to do that. He wanted her then, but duty called and pursuing her would have been a distraction. Amusing and more than likely extremely fulfilling, but still a distraction. He didn't do distractions when his family needed him.

The sparkle in her eyes and the spirited way she shot back at him stoked the fire already burning in his gut. Few women would dare engage him in such a dispute. Obviously she didn't care. He liked that. Hypnotically he watched the smooth sway of her hips as she walked ahead with his grandfather. She had an apple bottom, just as he liked them, tight and firm. His hands itched to touch her there and everywhere else. This was going to be a long night.

His brief romances were quick and uncomplicated and both parties always parted satisfied. He'd had his share of romance, none particularly serious. He was too busy for serious. The understanding was always simple: physical only—no emotions. But unfortunately, emotions sometimes got in the way. When women got too clingy or wanted more than he intended to give, he very easily and quickly ended the union.

"Jacob, you have a call in the office," Bane said, finding them in the library. "It's Daniel, he wants to discuss tomorrow."

"I have to take that," Jacob said, "Andre, do me a favor

and show our beautiful guest around a bit. I'll meet you later in the dining room." He walked out. Andre turned to Jo and smiled.

"Shall we?"

Chapter 4

He led, she followed. They walked through the house mostly in a companionable silence. He paused with a brief description, then she'd peek in. The house was far larger than she thought. It came complete with a heated indoor swimming pool with retractable roof and a glass wall of windows showing the connected outdoor pool, basketball court, movie theater and solarium. When they arrived back at the two-story library, the tour ended.

She looked around at the mint-condition books as Andre walked over to the desk and opened the laptop. She watched as he pressed a few buttons, then a printer on the credenza activated. When the pages started printing he looked up at her.

"Tell me, Ms. Butler, what exactly do you expect to get out of all this?"

She'd been waiting for this. "What do you want me to tell you?"

"How about the truth?"

"Fine, the truth is I just want to do my job," she said. He walked over to the printer and grabbed the papers. "I presume this is when we do the legal jargon?"

"Very perceptive," he said, flipping through quickly before handing them to her. She took them as he picked up a pen from the desk. "It's a standard nondisclosure agreement. The terms are nonnegotiable. Basically all intellectual property obtained in the process of your employment here is the express property of the Titan Corporation. Whatever you find, uncover or learn stays here. No exceptions. This contract can also be dissolved for any reason." She didn't look at the papers. She just took the offered pen and signed. "Trusting?"

"Confident," she said, handing the signed pages back to him. "I don't get it, what exactly is your problem with me? Do we know each other aside from the airport earlier?"

"No."

"Then what is it?"

"My job is to plan for the worst. You're an unknown, that makes you a threat."

"What does that mean? How am I a threat to anyone?"

"It means that I'd rather not have to deal with you and my grandfather in the near future," he said.

She looked at him, confused by his remark, and then it hit her exactly what he was suggesting. "If you're saying what I think you're saying, then you're kidding me, right? Me and Jacob? He is old enough to be my grandfather too."

"That hardly matters, does it?" he said.

"Maybe not for some, but it does to me. Look, your grandfather is a sweet man, he's interesting, and his business sense is brilliant. I admire that, but that's it. That's as far as it goes. He's not exactly my type when it comes to my personal life."

"I've heard that before."

"I realize this family has had problems in the past. I've recently read about them. I've even read about Jacob's occasional liaisons, and yes, I'm no fool, there are women who would love nothing better than to hook up with a man like your grandfather. But I'm not one of them."

"Again, I've heard that before," he said dryly. "My grandfather is no fool, but he does like the attention of attractive young women. Unfortunately that attention often comes with a high price. My job is to protect my family, even from themselves."

"But not from me. I'm not a threat. Obviously there's no way I can prove to you that I'm not here to cause trouble, so you can either take my word for it or not. I was hired to help Jacob complete his bio and that's what I intend to do."

"I wouldn't get too comfortable in that resolve."

"I'm writing the Jacob Buchanan biography," she said stubbornly.

"No one is writing a Buchanan biography."

"You're not seeing the big picture. Imagine all the aspiring businessmen out there. Your grandfather is a legend, a role model. The sum of his experiences is priceless. He's an incredible man with a fascinating story to tell. I would think you'd be honored to have others know that. People would be fascinated to read his life story."

"People are fascinated reading tabloid trash, that's hardly motivation for me to hand my family over to them with a bow on top. So you've obviously discussed publication with him?"

"I view any discussion with Jacob regarding this venture as confidential."

"Have you shopped proposals?" he asked more pointedly. She didn't answer. "Silence is often a sign of admission."

"What are you so afraid of? Whatever was done was done in the past. Your persistent defensiveness makes me think this family really does have secrets to keep," she said.

"The only thing this family wants to keep is our privacy. We've had outsiders come here before. They all have the same ulterior motives, reporters wanting a story, business associates wanting inside information, so-called friends wanting favors and of course lovers using their position wanting whatever they could get. Why shouldn't I think you do too?"

"I can't stop you from thinking whatever you want. But I know the truth," she said.

"The truth is in my experience most writers usually come with a false assumption. They either try to prove it legitimately, fabricate questions to have the reader draw certain conclusions or they manufacture evidence to prove it to justify their assumption."

"Obviously you haven't come in contact with many writers."

"On the contrary, I deal with writers all the time."

"You're in PR, you deal with the media, that's different."

"Writers nonetheless," he shot back.

"Writers with a time sensitive deadline and in need of scintillating copy to sell papers," she said. "That's not me. I'm not a fiction writer or tabloid newspaper writer. I'm a biographer. I write factual information, plain and unadulterated. I simply state facts. I arrange them in a cohesive order and present it in a logical articulate form. So if you're trying to get into my head and shrink me out, don't waste your time."

"What makes you think I'd do that?"

"I do my homework too," she snapped, feeling her integrity being questioned again. Anger began to swell. She had no intention of putting up with another round of character assaults.

"You're exactly as I expected."

"And how is that?" he asked.

"Coldhearted, closed-minded and self-absorbed," she said.

"I'm glad I didn't disappoint," he said calmly.

"Hardly, but it wasn't like I was expecting a Hallmark moment. You might think the Buchanan men are God's gift to womanhood and have hordes dropping at your feet, and you might be right, but you can rest assured I'm not one of them. No disrespect intended. I came here to do a job for a client, not to fight with the client's grandson. Now if you'll excuse me, I need to find Jacob." She turned to walk out of the library.

"A few words of advice—keep your bags packed. But I suppose as an opportunist, you already know that."

She stopped and turned around. She knew exactly what he was implying. It was a direct hit on her integrity and it was all she needed to tell him exactly what she thought of him and his implication.

She smiled. "You don't scare me Buchanan," Jo said, as she moved closer. Wanting to make no mistake, she needed him to hear and understand every word she said. "I've dealt with men like you all my life. You throw your money and power around and expect everyone to do exactly as you want. You don't ask, you order. You take what you want by force, by threats or otherwise. Well, not with me, not this time. I don't run away from anyone, not anymore. You can't move me. So you can do whatever it is you intend to do, because I'm not leaving until this job is done." When she finished she stiffened her back and glared up at him almost daring him to counter. He did, although not as she expected.

Andre smiled at her defiance. There was a spark of passion and fire in her eyes as she spoke that set his body on fire. Few women had the audacity to provoke him like this. He had to admit, he liked it. As a matter of fact if they were in a different situation he might have even enjoyed taking her up on her dare.

"No reply?" she challenged.

Adrenaline levels that had already spiked were now teetering on the edge for both of them. He smiled, enjoying the obstinate spunk she showed. Even now after everything he assumed about her, she still excited him. He could see the excitement and arousal in her eyes as well. "And you can skip the charm, I'm not buying it."

His smile broadened as he admitted the truth to himself. From the moment he saw her, his instant attraction was irresistible. He had never felt anything like this before. "You can lie to me, but not to yourself, Ms. Butler," he said smoothly, as he took a step closer to her. "You want me right now just as much as I want you. But know this—I will not confuse this attraction with my obligation to protect my family."

She stepped back and squared her shoulders. He obviously knew which buttons to push, because he was right, she did want him. But she'd never admit to it. "Your conceit knows no bounds, does it?"

"Don't you," he baited her, "want me?" He licked his lips seductively. She didn't respond. His eyes focused on the lusciousness of her full coral mouth. The slight quiver gave him his answer. He smiled, satisfied with the simple gesture.

"No," she lied.

He chuckled. His response came almost instantly. Without thought, he reached out, grabbed her waist, pulled her to his body and kissed her.

In an instant her body went limp. Her heart slammed

against her chest as she was scooped into his arms. It had been too long and her body was reacting fast.

Initially, she was too stunned to move, he literally took her breath away. Her lips were already parted, so he took advantage and inserted his tongue. His body turned and pressed her against the back of the sofa and she felt his hardened erection. His strong arms encircled her and she him. It took her a few seconds to realize what was happening. She continued kissing him back, then on the brink of losing control, she pushed him away, fire flaring in her eyes. Her mouth was still open in shock. She held her hand to his chest to hold him back while it took a few seconds for her to catch her breath. "Are you insane? You can't just walk up and kiss somebody like that."

"If I'm not mistaken, Ms. Butler, you kissed me back."

"Don't flatter yourself. I didn't have much of a choice.

"That's why you enjoyed it."

She did and he knew it. The victorious expression on his face made her want to punch him. She opened her mouth to speak but stopped when she heard Jacob's voice behind them. She turned. "Ah, there you are, dinner's ready," Jacob said as he walked into the library. He looked at Jo's flushed expression. "Everything okay in here?" he asked.

She nodded slowly. "Yes, fine, I just need to wash my hands."

Chapter 5

With ceiling lights slightly dimmed, tapered candles glowing and fresh flowers everywhere, the large formal dining room was exquisite. Jo looked around and smiled, amazed by the elegance of her surroundings. The twelve seat table was covered with a brilliant white linen cloth and adorned with fine china, Waterford crystal and polished silver. "Wow," she said softly as she entered the room.

"Ah, there you are. Come, have a seat," Jacob offered as he and Andre stood when she approached. Andre walked around and held her chair out for her. She sat while looking at her place setting. A small salmon, dill and caviar platter sat beside her plate. Her stomach rumbled softly. Jacob nodded to the server who immediately grabbed a bottle and poured champagne into each of their glasses.

"A toast, to our lovely guest," Jacob raised his glass and smiled, "I hope your time with us is pleasant and fulfilling." Jo blushed and nodded then held her glass up to him and then to Andre, who surprisingly was smiling and nodding in agreement. Moments later the meal was served. Lobster bisque was first then a baby leaf salad with vinaigrette dressing. Next came beautifully prepared crab-stuffed tilapia with asparagus and new potatoes.

An hour later the meal had come to an end. Dinner had been delicious and the conversation was lively and amusing, thanks solely to Jacob. They sat at the dining room table as coffee and dessert were served. Jacob kept the mood light talking about his life and his career, his hopes and dreams for the future.

Jo had no idea that he went to work for his father and never finished high school. He eventually got his GED and went to college. As a result he insisted that his children each get a master's degree. While creating Titan Energy, he worked fourteen hours a day, seven days a week and kept that schedule until the day he retired. As for his future dreams, he wanted Titan out of the oil business and into the energy business.

Jo listened attentively, enjoying his stories and memories, each one more entertaining than the last. She tried to remember most of them so she could ask questions about them later. The last thing she wanted to do was begin taking notes. She needed to earn trust and that wasn't the way to do it.

She made comments, but was careful not to ask too many questions during the meal. She knew Andre would be paying particular attention, so she decided to begin slowly and take her time. If this was going to work she needed the cooperation of everyone involved, including Andre and the rest of the family. She had a feeling they'd be just as closed off as he was.

Jo glanced at Andre from time to time as Jacob spoke. His reactions were reserved. He seemed pensive and withdrawn. Whatever was on his mind had completely consumed him. Even when Jacob included him in the conversation, he commented briefly then that was it. By the time coffee and dessert were finished, it seemed he'd completely shut down, which was just fine with her. She'd rather not have to deal with him anymore. One interaction was more than enough.

If his intent was to knock her off balance with the kiss, then he had certainly done it. She was off balance. As a matter of fact, she was still reeling. She hated to admit it, but she had enjoyed it. Of course maybe that was because she hadn't been kissed in months. Fine, he'd gotten to her once, there was no way she was going to let him rattle her again.

"Ms. Butler," Andre said suddenly, calling her by her last name and catching her off guard again. She turned her attention to him. "I have a few questions I'd like to ask if you don't mind."

"Sure," Jo said placing her cup back on the saucer.

"Why don't you tell us about yourself?" he asked.

She looked at him trying not to look as surprised as she was and also to gauge his intent to figure out what he was up to. "Okay, sure, I went to University of Pennsylvania and majored in English. I worked for a publishing company after I graduated then a few years ago I started writing freelance. I grew up in Florida and now live in New Jersey."

"And your family?" he asked.

"I'm an only child, no brothers, no sisters, no family. I was placed in foster care since birth. I lived with a few different foster families. When I was about twelve years old I started running away repeatedly. I was eventually permanently placed back in foster care. I stayed there until I graduated from high school, after that, college and work. That's about it, except that I'm looking forward to working on this project."

"Do you write a lot of biographies?" Andre asked.

"I used to."

"You used to?" Andre asked, "Why'd you stop?"

"What I meant is that I haven't written a biography lately, at least not for a while," she tensely, looking over to Jacob and smiling, "but yes, I have written several in the past," she said, knowing that Andre noticed her reaction.

"When was your last biography assignment?"

"A little over a year and a half ago," she said.

"Interesting," he surmised quickly, "isn't that unusual for a writer who professes to write bios? I mean that seems like a long time between jobs. You couldn't find work in a year and a half?"

"I'm selective with my projects."

"You must be. So who was your last bio?"

"I wrote a bio for a U.S. politician."

"Which politician?" he asked.

"I'm not at liberty to say at this time," she said, hoping he would infer that her client wanted the bio kept quiet and not the real truth of the situation.

"Did you go to this unnamed politician's home? Is that the usual procedure, to stay in a client's home?"

"In most cases yes, I interview the client and family members. All cases vary. I gather whatever documentation they have, plus do in-depth research according to how detailed the biography and the desired result."

"Desired result?" Andre asked.

"Not everyone wants their bio published for the general population to read. Some just want to do a family history for future generations to enjoy."

"Jo, why don't you tell Andre about the other things you write," Jacob said. "Tell him about your column."

"I write a monthly column for a women's magazine."

"It's very popular," Jacob said, "you should check it out.

There's talk of having it syndicated in several major newspapers across the country."

"Perhaps I will," Andre hedged.

"It actually gave me a few ideas to try out," Jacob added.

"Ideas, really," he said. "What kind of column is it?"

"It's a relationship column," she said, seeing his brow arch with interest. She really didn't want to get into a discussion about the column. "I've also written quite a few other pieces for newspapers and magazines."

"Anything I might have read?" Andre asked.

"I doubt it. Most of them are smaller pieces."

"Ah, now she's being modest. One of Jo's so-called 'smaller pieces' was nominated for a very prestigious award."

"Impressive," Andre said, genuinely impressed.

"Indeed. I think she's the perfect person to help complete my biography. It needs a fresh eye, she's got it."

"I'm really excited to continue this project, Jacob. I read everything you sent me and I do have some questions and some ideas. I guess we can get started first thing tomorrow if that's okay with you."

"Fine, sounds perfect," Jacob said happily.

"Actually, Granddad, you have an important meeting tomorrow in Anchorage," Andre said interrupting. "Dad's sending the helicopter in the morning."

"Ah yes, nearly slipped my mind again. Well, my dear," he said regretfully, "I'm afraid I'm going to have to leave you in my grandson's very capable hands for the next few days. I need to get back to Anchorage. Duty calls."

"Oh, I'm sorry to hear that," Jo said, not hiding her disappointment. "I was looking forward to getting started tomorrow."

"Oh, we'll get started soon enough, don't worry about that." Jacob reached out to take her hand and squeezed it gently. "You just stay put and I'll be back in no time. Meanwhile, I'm sure Andre here will take good care of you," Jacob said. Andre looked across the table at his grandfather holding Jo's hand. Neither spoke. But they both had the same stoic expression. "He can be a bit stiff," Jacob continued with a wink to his grandson, "so don't pay him too much mind. He takes life too seriously that's all."

"Granddad…"

"Don't granddad me now. You need to loosen up and live a little. Get out of the office and smell the roses as it were. I've got an idea. This is Jo's first time in Alaska. Why not give our guest the grand tour of Juneau?"

"That's not necessary, Jacob, really," Jo said. "I'll be fine while you're away. I have plenty to keep me busy and I'm sure your grandson is a busy man. The last thing he has time to do is baby-sit me."

"Nonsense, it'll do you both some good. Andre can also give you a bit of history about Titan."

"I'll be fine, really," she reiterated.

"Well, you're going to need to see Juneau eventually. It's my hometown, where I was born and raised. Alaska is an important part of our family history. You should visit some of the important places; get the flavor so you can write a more accurate description."

Jo smiled then glanced at the glaring man sitting across from her. It was obvious this wasn't his idea and being stuck with her was the last thing he wanted. She suddenly smiled. The thought of annoying Andre seemed to all of a sudden not be such a bad idea. "Okay," she finally agreed. Andre glared at her. She continued smiling.

"Good, now that that's settled, I'm going to call it a night." He stood and walked around to stand beside her chair. Jo pushed her chair back slightly. "No, sit, stay awhile, I insist, enjoy your coffee and dessert." She slowly sat back down. "You two can chat about tomorrow. I've got an early morning appointment with a helicopter and a bit of packing to do. Jo, if you need me I'll be at my Anchorage house. Good night," he said, grasping her hand and kissing it.

"Good night, Jacob," she said happily.

"Good night, Granddad," Andre said, still staring at her.

"Good night, grandson." Jacob said, and then left Jo and Andre sitting at the dining room table.

Jo pushed her chair back from the table. "Actually I think I'm going to get some work done," she said. "Good night."

"No wait, stay, please," Andre said.

She paused before standing and looked at him. "Round two? I'm not in the mood. Maybe some other time."

"No, nor am I. Look, you and I will be working together for the next few days. We need to resolve this."

"Maybe you should speak to your grandfather," she said.

"I will, in time. But right now I want to apologize for my behavior earlier. Seeing you in the airport and then here at the house took me off guard. The kiss was impulsive."

"Apology accepted, good night," she said.

"Wait, I'm sorry you've come all this way for nothing."

"I wouldn't say it was for nothing. Your grandfather is a legend. His story is inspiring and Titan is…"

"Titan is just a small family-owned company," he interrupted. "We explore and develop energy possibilities. That's all."

She smiled. "I'd hardly call Titan a small family-owned company. Titan Energy Corporation has been growing steadily for the past seventy-five years. I've read your last few annual reports and quarterly financial news bulletins. They were very informative, although surprisingly they were missing something."

"Which is?" he queried with interest.

"You show numbers, ratings, assessments, everything, while still lacking any detailed information on its owners, the Buchanans. The Internet has over a million notations for Titan and Buchanan yet there's nothing anywhere that chronicles Louis's or Jacob's life. Don't you think people are interested? It's quite the smoke and mirror show."

"We have limited shareholder attachments, less than twelve percent holdings. Believe me, they're only interested in making money. They don't care who's behind the curtain pulling the strings and doing the dirty work."

"May I quote you on that?" she asked.

He chuckled, stood and walked to the buffet table. "Nicely done," he said, then brought a presentation folder and handed it to her.

She eyed it suspiciously, not knowing what to expect. "What's this, more legal papers to sign?"

"I thought I'd save you some trouble," he said, handing her a PR overview of Titan.

She opened the folder and flipped though several pages, articles, photos, charts and PR material. She pulled one sheet out and read it aloud.

Family-owned and operated since 1902, Titan Energy Corporation is a majority privately owned company with minor tradable interests with concerns in natural gas, minerals, and oil production and exploration. The Company has undergone major transitional phases. Named Buchanan Mining Company Limited in 1900, it was originally established as a gold mining and supply company in the early nineteen hundreds.

Recently the Company is engaged in oil exploration and mineral mining. In 1966 the Company name was changed to Titan Energy Corporation. Under the steady leadership of Jacob Buchanan, Titan Energy Corporation has continuously emerged as a vital contender in the future of international energy.

"Wow," she said dryly as she looked at him across the table from her. "Very convenient, Mr. Buchanan."

"I aim to please," he said, his eyes held hers transfixed.

"This is exactly what I needed, a pre-approved press folder. Gee whiz, wish I hadn't come all this way. You could have just faxed this to me and saved me the trouble."

"Sarcasm," he said amused.

"Ya think?" she mocked, tilting her head with enjoyment.

He smiled tensely then stood and walked to the buffet table again. She was getting under his skin in more ways than one. "Let's not insult each other's intelligence, so I suggest we get to the point. What exactly do you want to end this, Ms. Butler?" He picked up the bottle of wine, walked back to the table and stood beside her.

"I want to do my job, do what I was already paid to do."

"Paid, fine. In that case keep the money and go."

"I'd rather keep my integrity and just do the job."

"I'll give you a very nice bonus. I'm sure your integrity will be fine with a few added zeros." He filled her wine glass slowly then leaned down, tilted his head to speak directly in her ear. "What do you think?"

She shivered as she felt the heat of his breath against her ear and neck. The conversation had taken a whole different tone. Not realizing he was as close as he was, she turned to face him. They were just inches apart. "I think if I didn't know better, I'd say you were trying to bribe me."

"I guess it's a good thing you know better," he said softly, moving closer still.

He seemed to dare her to retreat. She didn't. "Do I?" she whispered boldly as she looked into his eyes. Her heart slammed against her chest. He smiled. Then in an instant his mouth descended and captured hers—literally taking her breath away. The kiss, hesitant at first, quickly became demanding, as he pressed her solidly against the back of the chair. She felt his tongue press to her lips, she opened to him. He tilted his head and delved deep into her mouth and she into his. They tasted each other with probing delight. A rush of sensual excitement raced through her body, turned her inside to molten lava.

Her senses swam, befuddled and bewildered, drinking in the sweet nectar of his mouth. Someone moaned, or perhaps they both did. The surging intertwining dance of tangled tongues increased, as did their burning desire. Her heart raced—pounding like drums against her chest. Her nerves tingled and a place in the pit of her stomach trembled and shook. This wasn't just a kiss, this was a message. He sent, she received and tried her best to send one of her own.

The kiss ended slowly with their lips barely touching. Breathless, with her heart beating rapidly, she looked at him. She refused to be rattled this time. "The writer in me might wonder why that is?"

He smiled realizing that she had continued their previous conversation before the kiss. He was impressed, she was good and there was nothing he enjoyed more than a challenge. "The writer in you might need an impressive reference. I'm sure a note scribbled on Titan letterhead would look impressive enough for your next client."

"But I'd still have to face myself in the mirror."

"You'll find it's a lot easier when the mirror is gilded."

"You're good," she said smiling slowly.

"I'm better than you can possibly imagine," he promised, moving in to kiss her again.

She leaned back. "Thanks, but no thanks," she said, sliding away on the other side of the chair then standing.

She stepped back, putting her empty chair between them. "I think the price is a bit out of my reach."

"Are you sure?" he asked, moving around the chair and caging her against the table. Breathless, she planted her hand on his chest for distance. She could feel his heart beating, matching her own rapid rhythm. He was obviously just as excited as she was. The simple intimacy seemed to suggest more. He took a step even closer. "Are you sure," he repeated, smiling a self-assured smirk that she quickly recognized as steeled confidence.

Jo smiled, realizing his ploy. "You're wasting your time," she said. "This charismatic charm thing that I assume works on your other conquests won't work on me. So you can put away your psychology degrees, I don't want to play your games."

"I don't play games." His tone softened, surrounding her in a sensual whisper. He raised her other hand to his lips and kissed her wrist. He felt her pulse quicken and her hand shake. "You're shaking."

"I'm cold," she lied poorly.

He shook his head, knowing the truth. "No. You see, your eyes tell a different story. Just like at the airport. You were searching for someone."

"Yes, I was looking for your grandfather."

"You might have been looking for my grandfather, but you found me."

She gasped silently. *How could he read her so well?* He knew exactly what buttons to push. And he was very good at pushing them. He was definitely right about one thing, he was better than she imagined. "You like this sparring tête-à-tête, don't you? Add a bit of lustful psychoanalyzing and you're right in your element," she said, her eyes burning into his with as much intensity as she could summon.

"We were attracted to each another from the start."

"Attractions can be suppressed."

"Can they?" he asked.

"Yes," she said quickly, although not as convincingly as she hoped. His eyes sparked. They both knew she was lying.

"Not this one," he replied more definitively.

She didn't answer. She was out of sassy comebacks and quick cutting retorts. She just stood with one hand planted on his chest and the other in his hand. He was right about everything. She did want him then as much as she wanted him now. They stood face-to-face for a moment, neither spoke. The more they gazed into each other's eyes, the stronger the pull became.

He leaned in, she leaned up. In an instant their mouths connected a second time. Filled with passion and desire, the slow sensuous kiss erupted into lustful hunger. She wrapped her arms around his neck as his hands enveloped her body pulling her close. Now, pinned firmly against the table, the kiss absorbed them both.

Jo opened her mouth, accepting him into her warmth. Their tongues danced passionately, tasting and savoring the sweet fragrance of each other. His arm encircled her, pulling her even closer while his unmistakable erection pressed against her. His hand fell to her breast, gently kneading, caressing and massaging the rounded fullness beneath the cashmere sweater. She moaned in his mouth, he groaned in hers.

Her rational mind shattered. Desire and passion replaced all reasonable thought. Her want was too strong and his seductive pull was too tempting. As the kiss deepened and his sinful hands touched her, she swam in the possibility of her awakening passion. Yet, she knew this was wrong. But it felt so right. He made her body burn and she loved it. The fiery kiss ended with scorching nibbles down her neck. She closed her eyes, bathed in the radiance of his intensity. She shuddered and gasped when his tongue licked her earlobe then suckled it. Right here, right now, she wanted this, she wanted him.

"Let's go," he muttered breathlessly, taking her hand.

She followed for a few steps then stopped. He turned to her. "No, I can't do this," she said pulling back. She turned and walked away.

"Are you sure?"

She didn't turn around. She wasn't sure if she could pull off another round with him. Leaving was her best bet. "Positive. Good night, Andre. I'll see you tomorrow."

Chapter 6

If he responded to her last remark she didn't hear it. She was too busy making a swift retreat—or was it just running away again? Up the stairs and down the hall, she didn't stop moving until she opened the bedroom door and closed it soundly behind her. She leaned back against the frame and took a few deep breaths. Her heart was beating wildly and her stomach had done so many flops she felt as if she'd just gotten off a corkscrew roller coaster.

Actually that's exactly what she'd done. Dueling with Andre was precisely that. She licked and touched her swollen lips savoring his lingering taste. "He kissed me. He kissed me," she whispered, in the empty room. "And I can't believe I kissed him back."

She didn't know what to make of it other than the fact that it was unbelievable. Salacious to the point of mind-blowing, the kiss had her toes curling and her pulse racing. The man definitely excelled in kissing, making it an art form. His touch had raised her inner temperature at least twenty degrees. She pushed away from the door frame and walked over to the bed. Sitting down she released the top few buttons on her cashmere sweater. She was suddenly hot all over her body.

She lay back on the bed looking up at the ceiling and shaking her head from side to side.

She needed to regain control and focus. This wasn't about Andre, this was about her. She needed to do this. She sat up and grabbed her charging cell phone. She called her friend, Pamela. She answered sleepily. "Hey, it's me."

"Hey, are you okay, did Jacob finally show up?"

"I'm fine," Jo said, "I'm at Jacob's house now, I met him here."

"So everything is as you expected?" Pamela asked.

"Not quite, but nothing I can't handle."

"What do you mean?" Pamela asked.

Jo took a deep breath and sighed. "Andre Buchanan is here."

"He's there at the cabin with you?" Pamela sighed also. "I figured he'd show up, but not this soon. So you met him?"

"Actually we met at the airport, but I didn't recognize him at the time."

"How could you have not recognized that man?"

"Easy, I haven't seen his face in two years and then he wore a beard. I stopped working on Jacob's bio so there was no need for me to look him up again until now. Besides, I was focused on Louis and Jacob, not Andre. I know he's in the news all the time, but energy and oil isn't exactly my interest, so no, I didn't recognize him."

"I can believe that."

"Anyway, apparently he doesn't like the idea of me being here alone at the cabin with Jacob or even helping him write his memoir. You've met him, right? What's your impression of him?"

"Yes, we met a few years ago and then again recently when we were bailing my mother and his grandfather out of jail. Don't ask," she said before Jo could interrupt. "Anyway, he was a lot nicer before his grandmother died and before his two-week marriage a year ago. Now he's devoted everything to protecting the family. He's almost obsessive about protecting his family, especially his grandfather. I'm sure it has a lot to do with the interior designer, the waitress and the stripper thing last year with Jacob. Remember, Jacob stayed in the tabloids with those women for weeks."

"But they were obviously gold diggers. They wanted Jacob for his money. I just want to finish this job as promised."

"Oh yeah and who can forget the aspiring actress, what's her name. Seriously, I can totally understand him being suspicious."

"Yeah, but not every woman who comes to Alaska is after the Buchanan men and their money."

"But there are enough that are."

"Well, I was already forewarned that the rest of the family might resist at first. So I guess I should feel honored that they pulled out the big guns for me."

"Honored isn't exactly the word I would go for," Pamela said.

"It doesn't matter, I can handle whatever he's got. He can take his best shot," Jo assured her.

"Do you hear yourself? Girl, you need to be careful, this is serious. He specializes in manipulation. I hear he's even more lethal to the heart than you are, and now that's saying something." She chuckled at her humorous remark.

"Not very funny," Jo said sarcastically.

"Seriously, if anything, you and he should get along just fine because both of you have emotional attachment issues."

"I do not."

"Please, you both have that detached commitment-phobic 'one date and they're toast' thing going on."

"See, now you're just exaggerating, I'm not that bad. But getting back to the point, I'm not here to get involved with him or anyone else. I'm here to finish the job I started two years ago and then leave. As for Andre, he could go tonight and it would be fine with me."

"Then why do you sound troubled?" she asked. "Did something already happen?"

"We kind of already had an altercation."

"What did he do, offer you money to quit the job?"

"Yes, and other things," she said.

"What other things?"

"He kissed me," Jo blurted.

"Did you just say that he kissed you?" Pamela asked.

"Don't ask. Just trust me, I can handle this. I gave my word and I'm keeping it. As a matter of fact, I think I'm going to get started and work on a few things before I turn in tonight."

"No way, I want to hear more about this kiss."

"There's nothing to tell," Jo said trying not to think about him or the memory of the feel of his body pressed to hers. "It was no big deal. He just caught me off guard. That's all." His lips were soft and firm as his hard body pressed her against the back of the library sofa.

"No big deal, huh," Pamela said, "I bet you're thinking about him right now."

"Then you'd lose," Jo lied, hoping her friend couldn't tell. "I'm thinking about jumping rope in the snow." She blurted out the first thing to pop into her head. It was totally ridiculous, of course.

"Liar," Pamela said, while laughing. Seconds later, Jo joined her. The truth was too obvious for them to deny.

"Fine, whatever, for real it was a big deal. But don't worry about me. I can handle this," Jo affirmed. "I'll e-mail you tomorrow to keep in touch."

Pamela yawned. "Sounds good, what time is it?"

"Late. Four hours makes a lot of difference. Go back to sleep. Good night." Jo closed her cell ending the call. She didn't exactly lie to her friend as much as omit some of the truth. Everything was all right, to a certain extent, wasn't it? Andre was just a momentary distraction that she was sure she could handle. Couldn't she?

She'd read about Andre as she'd done with the other notable members of the Buchanan family. He was very good at his job and his manipulation skills were well-known. When a family member staggered into the limelight, he effectively turned it off. She read about how he had spun his brother's situation with the sexual harassment case. It was brilliant. Paying for the plaintiff's mental health care was the perfect public relations solution. He expertly twisted, maneuvered and bent the public's perception to his will.

The thing was, he was doing the same thing with her. She'd fallen under his spell even before she knew who he was and now knowing him only made her want him more. Her reaction was surprising even to her. He was right. Their attraction wasn't going to be suppressed as easily as she hoped.

When it came to his job at Titan, as far as the public was concerned they were a small energy company servicing the general public. Few knew that their market value was in the billions and their public offerings were selling modestly. When Jo read that she actually laughed out loud. How could anyone believe that? It was proof of the power of his persuasion.

She could definitely see that. The man had a way of

bending people to his will. But she was just as willful and obstinate. Jacob hired her to finish a job and that's exactly what she intended to do. He wasn't going to change her mind about being here no matter what happened and how much he tempted her.

So what if it had been a while since she had time to relax and enjoy life in any measure? So what if the year had been stressful and she'd gone from job to job nonstop? She'd been focused and driven. She needed to do that again. Her last biography client had weakened that resolve and she needed to get it back.

Jacob wouldn't be here tomorrow. Fine, she needed to get started without him. She didn't need Andre for this. She glanced at the clock on the mantel. It was late, but she didn't feel particularly tired. She got up, unclasped then slipped her bra through her sleeve. The complete freedom of that simple act always made her feel better.

She looked at the two boxes Jacob mentioned earlier. They were sitting under the desk against the wall. She grabbed her briefcase from beside the bed and sat down at the desk. Pulling out cords, she set up her laptop and waited for the system to boot up. The house had wireless access, so when she clicked on the Internet icon, it popped up instantly.

She typed in "Titan." Several million hits appeared including those referencing Greek mythology and the moon of Saturn. She refocused her search to Andre Buchanan—Titan Energy Corporation. With that, several hundred thousand hits appeared. Before scanning the most promising, she scrolled the arrow up and clicked on images. A split second later images and still photos of the company and family appeared, including the one she remembered of Andre two years ago. He sported a close shaven beard. No wonder she hadn't immediately recognized him at the airport. He looked much younger clean shaven. She clicked on image after image after image. Andre's handsome face smiled back at her each time.

As PR director, he would more than likely be an excellent source of information. Unfortunately, he didn't exactly trust her. But she was used to that and had always changed minds. She found that people easily talked about themselves and their families given the right persuasion.

She knew she needed to open up and give more of herself before she could expect him to trust her. She was sure Jacob trusted her. Andre was a whole other story. "How do I resist you?" she asked the screen.

You can only be expected to be cool and nonchalant for so long and Jo had just about reached her limit. She played his game, but he was so much better at it. Pretending that the kiss she and Andre shared was meaningless? The man's mouth should be labeled a lethal weapon. Jo closed her eyes and took a deep breath. "Enough," she said and then went to work.

Andre stood leaning back against the table for a while. He didn't know what made him do what he did. All he knew was that he wanted her and a simple kiss wasn't going to do it. He wasn't fooling himself any more than he knew she wasn't fooling herself. They both knew that their attraction had taken on a life of its own. The desire and passion that surged between them wasn't just going to be ignored as she so naively put it. It was too strong and she was too tempting and according to everything he felt, she also was too willing.

But something held her back. He focused on a small segment of their conversation pertaining to how she worked *now*, as opposed to *before*. Her body language was very telling. She was nervous and defensive. He gathered that something major had happened for her to change her procedure. If he was going to do his job and protect his family, he needed to know what that something was. Maybe that something, if used to his advantage, was his in to getting her out.

He retired to his grandfather's office, sat at the desk and began an extensive search on Joanna Butler and her business. He scanned the usual sites, examining both business and personal information. There wasn't a lot of either and what was there was negligible. There was nothing particularly unusual about what she did or how she did it. She had an impressive list of clients with enough notable recommendations and testimonials to impress him, but that's not what he needed to see. He kept searching.

An hour later he gave up. Frustrated, but not discouraged, he drafted a quick e-mail to his associate, Ben Rhames, requesting more detailed information. Ben was a professional at finding what couldn't be found and with enough money he'd dig all the way back to Jo's roots. He found an image of her and dropped a copy of it into the e-mail then pressed Send.

It wouldn't be long until he had a full dossier on Joanna Butler with particular interest in her personal life first and then her business life. He closed out the file he began amassing on her and turned to work-related items. He read a few not-so-urgent e-mails, composed a few press releases and then found that his focus was waning. "Enough," he said, closing window after window until only one image appeared.

A wry smile tipped his lips as he stared at the photo left on the monitor. Jo smiled back at him. Her original image appeared from the copy he sent out to his associate. He stared at it until the eerie ghostlike fluidness of his aurora borealis screen saver spiraled listlessly. He watched with lackadaisical interest and amusement.

She had held her own against him. That in itself was admirable. He wasn't the easiest person to maneuver around. He was admittedly intimidating, shrewd and manipulative. He specialized in evading issues and controlling perceptions to his advantage. Reflecting, he reached up and touched his lips. It had been hours, but the feel of her was still there.

The kiss was an impulse, but it was something he had wanted to do since seeing her at the airport. His intention was to shake her up knock her off balance. But it seemed she had had the same effect on him. He turned his attention back to his work. He spent the next hour engrossed in business matters. He buried himself, but all attempts to erase Jo from his thoughts failed. She was always there in the background.

The women he had dealt with yielded to him in all things. He'd gotten used to being in control. So the idea of a woman challenging him gave him pause. He liked it— or maybe he was just tired. He decided to take care of this situation tomorrow. He went upstairs to his bedroom but noticed the light still on in the guest room. Weighing his options, he knocked.

Jo cracked the door open and gazed out at the man standing there. Andre stood with his head lowered. She didn't say anything, just waited for him to say what he came to say. He looked up, letting his eyes slowly drift up her body. He didn't smile.

"I saw that your light was still on," he began. She nodded. "I'm sorry. I didn't mean to imply that you were anything other than who you are. I guess I'm so used to putting out fires and avoiding scandals that I see a threat everywhere, even when it's not there." She opened the door slightly wider as he continued. "You're obviously not who or what I expected. I won't lie to you and tell you that I agree or approve of this whole thing, I don't. My job is to protect my family."

"I'm not here to hurt your family," she said, peering out from the partially open door.

"My grandfather has been through a lot. My grandmother's death devastated him, more than most know or could even imagine."

Jo nodded. "Believe me, I would never hurt Jacob." He nodded and turned. "Andre, wait," she said, reaching out and touching his arm. He stopped and turned back to face her. "Look, I know I can be a bit closed off at times, well, most of the time. My friends tell me that I don't play well with others." She smiled. He did too, then looked away a bit troubled. "What?" she asked curiously.

"Nothing, I was just thinking about what you might have been like growing up. In kindergarten for instance, if you didn't play well with others that would make you pretty lonely."

"I manage," she said, knowing that he was getting too close again. "I prefer solitude."

"Preferable introvert in a solitary profession?"

"As I said, I manage well enough. Being in foster care afforded me the skill to stand being alone. I didn't have anyone in my life except myself, so that's who I relied on," she said. "But don't pity me."

"Hardly, I admire you."

"Don't assume you know me by how I appear psychologically."

"Your nature is to hide your feelings and push people away. I'd say you're very good at it. Do you ever just let go and enjoy the moment? Damn the consequences?"

"No. Never. I guess that's why I work as I do, I don't have to get close to anyone. I just do my job and move on."

"And that works?" he asked.

She nodded. "For me it does. It has to."

He nodded his acceptance. "Since apparently I'm unable to stop this—fiasco…" he said, reaching into his pants pocket and pulling out a flash drive, "I want a copy of everything written, in progress. Agreed?"

She looked at the offered drive in his hand. "No. No one sees my work in progress, not even Jacob. It's part of the original agreement. If you want to review a copy after it's complete, you'll have to discuss it with him."

"That's unacceptable."

"It's nonnegotiable," she said defiantly.

She stood up to him again. He smiled and nodded curtly, knowing that he would get around that point easily enough. "In that case, good night," he said, and then turned and walked to the bedroom directly across from hers.

Chapter 7

The discussion, heated at times, raged for more than an hour. Jacob was firm and unmoved by the arguments Andre presented. But that didn't mean Andre was going to stop trying. Hammering his point for the last fifteen minutes, Andre refused to give up. "Granddad, leaving this in my hands is out of the question. I have work to do, an office to get to. The grand jury suspended the subpoena after the spill, but they're still investigating. I can't just drop everything and baby-sit your latest project. You don't need a biographer, you don't need a biography."

"Ah, that's where you're wrong. This family needs to remember where it came from. That means going back and writing everything down once and for all."

"But to what purpose?" Andre stressed.

"Posterity, son, posterity. Future generations of Buchanans need to know their past—the good, the bad and the ugly. Your children and your children's children need to know it. That's why I am doing this," Jacob insisted. "I won't be around forever and when I'm gone, so is our true history. This way it will live on through the written word."

"Granddad, we know our history. Dad, Uncle James, Aunt Ruth and Uncle Arthur, my siblings and cousins, we all know. You've told us," Andre insisted.

"Things change as oral history is passed down. I need the truth to be told. I was there; I remember everything."

"But a memoir, you don't even know what she intends to write. She told me last night that no one sees the work in progress, in this case, not even the client."

"That's correct."

"You don't know what she's writing about you, you don't have any control over what goes into it and you don't see it until it's complete." Jacob nodded. "What if it gets out to the public?"

"We have nothing to be ashamed about."

"Perhaps you're forgetting our early history. The Buchanans didn't exactly begin squeaky clean, did they?"

"As with most modern-day families with means, no we didn't. And there's nothing wrong with accepting that. The past is the past."

"Granddad, not everyone thinks that way. What if buried ghosts come back to haunt us? It's not unheard of."

"Then we'll deal with it, if or when it happens. We have nothing to be ashamed or afraid of."

"It's not about shame or fear, it's about privacy, our privacy. Our family's past isn't open for others to scrutinize."

"She is lovely, isn't she?"

"What?" Andre asked, taken off guard by the sudden change of topic.

"Jo, she's a beautiful woman. She's got backbone and spunk. I like that. A woman with a brain in her head who can take care of herself, I like that about her. She's smart, enthusiastic and very attractive," Jacob said. "If I were a few decades or so younger…" Andre looked at his grandfather suspiciously. The words were familiar. The dread in his expression was unmistakable. "You're thinking of the interior designer, aren't you?" Jacob said.

"It is oddly similar. A woman comes to do a job for you and weeks later our attorneys need to step in. It's the exact same scenario."

"Not at all, this is totally different. Jo has no ulterior motives whatsoever."

"I guess we'll have to see about that." Andre was about to state another case when his cell phone rang. He sighed heavily, pulled it out and answered. After a brief conversation, he closed it and put it away. "That was Bane. The chopper picked him up at the airport. It's about five minutes out, we should get outside," he said to his grandfather.

Jacob nodded and grabbed his hat and coat. Andre grabbed his briefcase and followed. They went outside to the pad and waited. "Granddad…"

"No, enough, don't granddad me, make it work. Take her to Juneau and show her our world. I'm still the patriarch of this family and sole majority holder in Titan. I may be retired, but you work for me, remember? That said, this is a direct order from the chairman and CEO emeritus. Take the time you need until I get back. Just make sure to treat her well. That means do as she requests, give her what she wants, no questions asked. I want Jo comfortable and happy when I get back. That means none of your sly tricks or PR foolishness. Jo is here as my guest, remember that. I want this project to happen," Jacob said decisively.

The firmness of his speech left nothing to misinterpretation. Jacob was obviously not giving in on this point, that meant Andre couldn't insist she leave. So if this project were to fall through, it needed to be her decision with no obvious interference from him. Andre frowned. That wasn't likely to happen. Jo was too thrilled to get this bio together. A frontal assault was out of the question. This might be trickier than he anticipated.

"Ah don't look so miserable, my boy. I'm leaving a very lovely woman in your capable hands. Most men would be delighted to have such a task as keeping her happy. But I know you'll do me right and be a true Buchanan. You may find she's rather nice to have around, so don't hurt her."

"I have no intention of hurting her," Andre said.

"You know exactly what I mean, none of your psychological tricks."

"Of course not," Andre said smiling. The wind kicked up as the helicopter approached. Both men looked up as it landed smoothly on the pad. Jacob held his hat down as Bane and the co-pilot hopped out and hurried over. The co-pilot tipped his hat as he picked up Jacob's small bag and hurried back to the chopper.

Andre handed Bane his grandfather's briefcase and Bane gave him a thick dossier and several overnight packages and envelopes. They spoke for a brief moment then Bane helped Jacob to the backseat of the copter. With Jacob buckled and secured, the helicopter slowly took off leaving Andre to be a true Buchanan—as his grandfather requested.

When the helicopter was nearly out of sight Andre walked back to the house considering how he might get around his grandfather's explicit orders. But as he saw it, he had no choice but to play nice, at least for now. Once inside he went directly to his grandfather's office. He flipped through the stack Bane gave him, seeing nothing of major interest or immediate concern.

He sat heavily, disturbed by the words echoing in his

head; a true Buchanan. A true Buchanan was exactly what he was trying to avoid. A true Buchanan meant his great-grandfather, Louis Buchanan, with the name taken in 1883 after he ran away from the south where he was born. Louis Buchanan was also the same man who came to this land and lied, stole, cheated, connived and pillaged to get what they now call a legitimate business.

Andre looked down at the envelope his grandfather left for him to give to Jo. He opened it and looked inside. There was a copy of his birth certificate, marriage license and various other documents. There were notes and diagrams and even a few personal letters. Nothing that would appear too scandalous, so he decided to do as his grandfather requested and hand them over.

He sat back thinking about Jo again. A slow lustful smile tipped the corner of his lips. He remembered their kiss well. It damn near kept him up all night. Knowing that she was just across the hall from his bedroom was tempting, but he knew he had time to work on her.

Jacob had asked him to take care of her before he left. Help her with the job and show her Juneau. He smiled, remembering the conversation with his father the day before. Perhaps he would take his advice and step it up a notch. He needed to make it her decision to leave, anything less and his grandfather would never forgive him. He needed to do more than seduce her, he needed to charm her. He needed to open her heart so that she'd fall for him. And he needed it done quickly.

He glanced up at the ceiling above his head. A creak in the floorboard told him that she was up. He smiled again thinking that the next few days would certainly be interesting. He was definitely going to enjoy his time with her. He'd pour on the charm, seduce her and wrap this up before his grandfather returned.

He began forming a complete solution to his dilemma. What if they had an affair and she got emotionally attached to him? He knew women, they always claimed they don't want commitment, but eventually the sound of wedding bells would deafen them. Jo was probably like every other woman, emotional and easily susceptible to seduction. It just might work. The emotional onset just might rattle her enough to make her leave of her own accord.

He smiled, noting his problem almost solved. She didn't quite trust him so he had to change that quickly. But he was PR director for Titan, how hard could it be to do PR for himself?

He grabbed his cell and began making arrangements for the next few days. If this was going to work, he needed to prepare. Impressing her might not be as easy as with most women and this was too important to leave anything to chance. Fifteen minutes later he hung up his call to a delivery company, satisfied with his preparations. Just as he placed the cell on the desk it rang. There was a minor crisis at his office. He turned on the computer and went to work. Thankfully work completely consumed him for the next hour.

"Good morning."

Andre looked up to see Jo standing in the office doorway. She wore a soft bright red V-necked sweater and slacks with her hair pulled back and resting on her shoulders. She looked sexy, although he doubted that was her intention. He smiled admiringly as his body reacted. His grandfather was right about one thing. She was definitely beautiful. "Good morning. I didn't expect you up this early."

"I'm an early bird. I've already worked for a few hours this morning," she smiled and looked around the office curiously. "Is Jacob still around?"

"No. He left just after dawn. He's probably already in Anchorage by now," Andre said. Her disappointment was obvious. "He left you in my very capable hands, his words."

"So, where is everybody else? Where's Bane?"

"Bane left with my grandfather. Housekeeping will be here later this morning and the cook has the day off."

"I see, so we're here alone?" she asked.

"Is that a problem for you?"

"No, of course not," she said still standing in the doorway. "I have plenty to keep me busy today."

"Would you like to come in, have a seat?"

"No, I'm gonna grab some tea and get back to work." She backed up to leave.

"Wait." Andre picked up the envelope Jacob left her. He stood and walked over to her. "This is for you."

She took the large envelope. "What is it?"

"My grandfather asked me to make sure you got it."

"Oh, okay," Jo said, seeming to relax knowing that it came from Jacob. She opened the envelope and quickly scanned through the papers. "Great, this is good, I can definitely use these," she said mostly to herself.

"I'm sure he'll be pleased to hear that."

She continued looking though the papers. "Okay, these will do fine. Thanks." She turned to leave again.

"So, are you ready?" he asked.

"Ready for what?"

"I thought we'd head out now." She looked puzzled. "My grandfather mentioned taking you around Juneau last night at dinner, remember?"

"Oh, okay, sure."

"Excellent. Give me twenty minutes and I'll meet you at the front door. Oh, do you have comfortable hiking boots or something like that?" She nodded. "Good, put them on, we're going for a walk."

"A walk?"

He nodded. "I'll meet you in twenty minutes." He didn't wait for her response.

She went to her bedroom and changed, putting on more durable clothing and her hiking boots. She looked at herself in the mirror before leaving. She looked practical and perfect. She headed to the front door, opened it and stepped outside. A chilled blast of cold air hit her instantly, but it was the beauty of the day that knocked her socks off. She was overwhelmed by what she saw.

Having arrived late last night, this was her first time seeing everything in the daylight. Vibrant green and luminous blue were everywhere, in the trees, lawn and sky. There were snow-capped mountains in the far distance. "Wow," she whispered to herself. She'd never seen anything so magnificent. "Unbelievable."

She had a few minutes to wait for Andre so she walked down the path a bit. She turned to get a panoramic view. As she did she looked up at the massive cabin-like structure behind her. It was magnificent—plain and simple on the outside yet comfortably elegant on the inside. She pulled out her cell phone and snapped a few photos then texted Pamela and forwarded the photos, knowing that she'd love them. She added a quick message, closed her cell and looked at her watch. It was time to meet Andre.

Chapter 8

Twenty minutes later Jo stood in the foyer still waiting. Andre was nowhere in sight. Why was it that men considered their time far more valuable than hers? Generally speaking, it was the same every time she co-wrote with CEOs, political figures, military leaders, or someone famous. They all had the same arrogance.

She waited another five minutes wondering what was going on. She was just about to go back upstairs when she heard a muffled motor and horn beeping outside. She walked to the door, opened it and looked out. Andre was straddling a huge all-terrain vehicle.

He got off and dashed up the front steps to meet her. "Hey, sorry I'm a little late. I had to get gas. Ready?"

"You are kidding, right?"

"Come on, you'll be fine," he said.

"Sure, I'll be fine 'cause I'll be dead. Do you know the accident statistics for those things?"

He chuckled. "I'm an excellent driver," he promised.

"Good for you," she said, not moving an inch.

"Trust me," he said, holding his hand out to her. She looked down at the offered hand. Gloved, it didn't seem menacing, but neither did the snake in the garden with the apple she assumed. "Come on, I promised my grandfather that I'd take good care of you. I intend to do that. Promise."

Reluctantly she took his hand and climbed down the steps. He grabbed the spare helmet and handed it to her. She looked at it and grimaced, but still put it on. He put his helmet on, swung his leg over and got comfortable then turned to her. Her hesitation was obvious. She looked at him and shook her head. "Are you kidding me?" she yelled so that he could hear through the thick padded helmet.

He laughed and spoke softly. "No need to yell, I can hear you. There are microphones and speakers in the helmets."

Surprised to his hear his calm voice echoing through the speaker inside her helmet, she laughed. "Sorry, I've never been on anything like this before. I've never even ridden a horse."

"Maybe we'll try that later," he turned to look at her. She licked her lips nervously, seductively and his body tensed and hardened instantly. The effect she was beginning to have on him was growing, literally. He wasn't sure if that was a good thing or a troubling thing. "Just swing your leg over behind me and hold on. I'll take it from there."

Jo nodded and did as he instructed. Once on, she sat much higher than she expected. She placed her hands on his shoulders. "Where are the seat belts?" she asked.

"No seat belts, just hold on tight," he warned as he started the engine. Seconds later the vehicle took off with a jerk and sped down the driveway. She screamed and wrapped her arms around his body and leaned in close. The intimate action sent a shiver and fire into her stomach even as her heart thundered from the beginning of what she knew would be a bumpy ride.

The start of their outing was nothing like she expected. Yes, the ride was bumpy and she felt as if she'd be tossed off any minute, but the view was incredible. After the driveway they took a dirt road that led into a thicket-like forest. They drove down the dirt road for a while then turned and headed up around a curving mountain path.

The underbrush seemed to get thicker and thicker as they drove. He talked to her the whole time, telling her stories about the indigenous people who no longer lived in the area. He spoke of their customs, religion and their language, most of which had long since vanished.

"So there's nothing left of them?" she asked.

"Not exactly. Some moved on farther north away from the coming encroachment of miners and early settlers, others stayed and eventually died or were killed decades ago. Still, there are a few Tlingit people around." He said something she didn't quite understand.

"What was that?" she asked. He repeated it. It wasn't that she didn't quite hear what he said. It was that it was in a different language. "What language is that?" she asked.

"It's Na-Dené, spoken by the Tlingit." He said something else she didn't understand.

"So what did you say?"

"I'll tell you later."

She didn't respond and tried not to focus on his comment. Whatever he said had softened his tone and made her stomach shudder again. "So who does this land belong to now?" she asked.

He paused a moment before answering. "The Buchanans," he said as simply as he could, trying not to make it sound any more grand than it already was.

"You own all this?" she asked, feeling the vehicle slow.

"It's no big deal," Andre said, stopping and turning the engine off. He helped her off then got off himself and removed his helmet. She took hers off too. They looked around. "It's all trees, forest and underbrush. Not exactly a rolling metropolis or Fifth Avenue prime real estate."

"Yeah, but it's a mountain, right? How do you own a mountain?"

"Actually they're several." He held out his hand and helped her hike along a ragged path. They continued to chat about the people and the land as they began to climb, him first, her following with his assistance. They climbed near vertical hills and snaked through lush moss-covered terrain beneath a canopy of trees that shot into the sky. They climbed higher and higher until reaching a small crack in the lush greenery. Andre led the way, holding her hand to keep her from falling.

Eventually they came to a large clearing at what seemed to be the top of a hill. Out of breath, she looked around with her mouth open. She held her breath. It wasn't a hill. It was a mountain. It was the top of a mountain.

She turned around several times in breathless, speechless wonder. "This is definitely not New Jersey," she said.

Andre laughed. "No, Jo, I don't suppose it is." He watched with joy at her wonderment of the sight he so often took for granted. This was once one of his favorite childhood adventures, but now it was just something his family owned.

"How do you find something like this? This place, I mean. You don't just go for a walk and stumble onto the top of a mountain and all this incredible beauty, right?"

"My family and I used to come up here years ago.

Before the ATVs we'd run or ride our bikes or mopeds. The road is a bit rough now, but a while back this was our hangout. Actually it was also my father's hangout and quite possibly my grandfather's hangout as well. My brothers and sisters and I would bring sandwiches up here during the day, play football or tag or just hang out. At night when we'd come up here we'd…"

"Wait, how in the world did you find your way at night?"

"We'd only come when there was a full moon. We'd get up here and lie down and watch the stars or if we were lucky we'd catch the northern lights in the sky."

"The aurora borealis? For real?"

"Sure."

"Unbelievable. It must be magnificent to see, to watch. Something so naturally awesome must make you feel so small and insignificant."

He nodded, hearing the joy in her voice and seeing the delight in her eyes. It was working. "The first time you see it, you're amazed. You don't speak, you just stare in wonder. There's nothing in the world like it. The colors and movement leave you speechless. Actually there are people that are literally hooked on them. It's like an addiction."

"I can believe that."

"The Cree people saw them as dancing spirits. They're supposed to direct your path and lead you home. I don't know, maybe they were right. Perhaps they know something we don't."

"I've always wanted to see it. I can't even imagine the experience."

"Come on, if we're going to make it back to go out to dinner, we need to get off this mountaintop."

"Dinner? But it's only a little after nine o'clock in the morning."

Forty-five minutes later they were back at the cabin, cleaned up, changed and heading across the channel into the city. The Juneau, Alaska, Andre introduced to Jo was far different than the one she'd read about and researched. As soon as they got into town they stopped and ate an early lunch at one of the many seafood restaurants on the wharf. Then they toured Juneau. Afterward they walked along the waterfront and talked. Jo turned and looked up at the massive mountains. "Which one is which?"

Andre turned to see what she was talking about. "Mount Juneau is over there and Mount Roberts is there on the right. Roberts is higher by a few hundred feet." He added more, telling her about the downtown area and its history. They stopped and leaned against a rail looking out at the channel.

"This place is so incredible," Jo said looking around.

"Sounds like you like our Alaska."

"You know what, I think I do. It's really amazing here. Everything seems so right, like nothing could go wrong." She looked at him. It seemed his thoughts were miles away now. She smiled and touched his arm. "Hey, are you okay?"

He turned to her. "Yeah, I'm just surprised," he said.

"By what?" she asked, looking around.

He turned to her. "I'm surprised that I'm having a really good time with you. It's been a long time since I could say that. Most women I'm with tend to…"

"Yeah, I've read."

"Don't believe everything you read," he said, "I'm not the womanizer the media makes me out to be. But here with you, right now, it's different. I really enjoyed myself," Andre said, surprising himself with the truth. He did have a great time with her.

"I'll take that as a compliment," she said.

"As it was intended," he said nodding. "You're okay." He meant it. In truth, he really didn't expect to enjoy himself as much as he had.

"Thanks, you're okay right back." She smiled until he took her hand and looked into her eyes. A few seconds later she slipped her hand from his and looked away.

"What just happened, that was supposed to be a good thing," he informed her.

"I know, and it was. It's just that..."

He held his hand up. "No, let me guess, you don't trust."

"It's not about my trust issues, it's about losing control. For some reason it's too easy with you. Being here with you, it's unnerving. I *never* do this, get close to someone so soon. As a matter of fact I usually go out of my way to avoid connecting with people."

"But here you are."

"Yeah, how about that."

"Never?"

"Never. It comes naturally. Growing up I had a dozen or so placements in foster care, all disasters. My last foster mother was the queen of blind devotion. People took advantage of her and her husband walked all over her. She never stood up for herself. She surrendered and just took it. I promised myself that I'd never be like that. I've lived my whole life fighting against it."

"What about relationships?"

"I work hard and steadily, it doesn't give me a lot of extra time. Dating sits on the back burner, I assume for you too."

"Come on," Andre said pushing away from the rail. "Let's walk." The conversation was obviously getting uncomfortable for both of them. They continued walking until they came to an area heavily populated with tourists.

"Where did everyone come from?" she wondered out loud.

"Cruise ships must have disembarked," he said.

The crowds around them chatted noisily, snapped photos, laughed and generally enjoyed the sights. Andre and Jo mingled in as they went into shops and boutiques checking out the local wares. Jo purchased a few items and had two small sculptures shipped, one to Pamela and one to Pamela's mother, Lydia. Andre heard her give the names and addresses. When they left the shop he asked about it. "I didn't know you knew Lydia."

"She's my best friend's mother. She suggested I take this job in the first place. Apparently she and Jacob are good friends."

"Yeah, they are, too good sometimes."

"How do you mean?"

He relayed a story of running some serious PR tricks to prevent each of their names from winding up in the national tabloids. Jo roared with laughter imagining Andre pulling off that particular assignment. "You're even better than I imagined."

"Are we talking about our kiss from last night?" he asked.

"No, I'm talking about being better at manipulating situations to suit your wants. You're good, very good."

"Again, are we talking about last night?"

"You have a one-track mind, don't you" she said, playfully swatting at his arm.

He ducked away then reached out and grabbed her waist, pulling her close. He kissed her and she wrapped her arms around his neck as the kiss deepened with more passion. It ended when people around them started applauding.

Totally embarrassed, Jo turned to hurry away, but Andre held her hand to keep her beside him. He tucked his arm around her waist to hold her still. "Newlyweds, am I right?" an older woman with bleached blond hair and a tightly pulled face asked and answered her own question. Andre smiled but didn't reply. She was soon joined by a small gathering of her traveling companions. "How long has it been, you two together?" she asked.

"Not long. Yesterday, last night actually," he said, answering her truthfully.

"Aw, isn't that sweet? See, see, you hear what he said? I told you they were newlyweds. Just because they don't have rings on doesn't mean squat nowadays. It's all in the eyes. It's attraction, I know these things," she bragged to her group of companions.

"Look at her, she's so embarrassed. Mildred, why do you want to go and embarrass the poor thing like that? Leave 'em alone. Let 'em enjoy their honeymoon in peace."

"All right, all right, Gladys, well God bless you both and I hope you have a long, loving life together with a dozen kids who adore you. Not like me and my Monty, God rest his soul—the cheating louse."

"Thanks, ladies, have a great day," Andre said, as he began walking with Jo at his side. "Bye."

"Goodbye," Jo added sweetly as they walked away. She smiled, trying her best not to laugh out loud as she overheard more of their conversation.

"What a lovely couple. See, I told they were newlyweds, you didn't believe me. Maybe you should listen to me next time. I know love when I see it…"

"You know from nothing. *I* said they were newlyweds…"

"You saw, she's got that look…"

"I saw, he's got that look…"

Andre and Jo walked away quickly then burst out laughing. She swatted at him again, this time clipping his arm. "Why did you do that?"

"Do what?" he asked innocently.

"Tell her that we were newlyweds."

"I didn't tell her we were newlyweds. She assumed it and I didn't dissuade her assumption."

"That's terrible."

"That's PR. I won't lie, but if an assumption is made to my advantage, so be it. She assumed we were honeymooning, I let her."

"You enjoyed doing that. It's like a game for you, isn't it?" He smiled without answering her question.

"Why ghost writing?" he asked, changing the subject.

"What do you mean?"

"I'm sure you're a very talented writer. Why not get credit and recognition for writing your own work?"

"Believe it or not, I like the anonymity."

"But you're always in the shadows, so to speak. No one ever knows how good you are."

"Not always. There's one book that I share credit with the client. Other times the client gets all the credit."

"Who are these clients?"

"Legally I can't tell you that, but believe me, you'd really be surprised by the famous names and New York Times single digit bestsellers I've written. I've also penned a book that was later made into a TV movie."

"Have you ever written your own book?"

"Yes, I've written four books, but I use a pen name."

"Interesting, even your own work is hidden behind another name. You must be the only woman without an ego."

"I wouldn't say that. I guess it's just not important that my real name be on everything I write."

"You're an interesting case study."

"Is that what I am today, a case study? Still trying to find out what makes me tick or are you still trying to get rid of me. Which is it?"

"I already know what makes you tick," he answered her question, but as usual, not completely.

"Really, and what do you think you know about me?"

"You say you have no ego and having your name, your real name on books or magazine articles isn't important. I think it is. I think perhaps you want your name there, but a name of your choosing. Jo Butler is ambiguous. You said that you were raised in foster care. You have no roots, no past except one you create. You have no one to care for, no attachments.

"Therefore your name means little to you, almost like the real you doesn't exist yet. You don't have a clear past, and you can't see a future. That's why you write anonymous bios of people. You go from experience to experience never taking anything away. You close yourself emotionally and you've built a wall around your heart to protect yourself. But someday, Jo, that wall is going to crumble. Your heart will be vulnerable and you're going to have to decide what you want, a future with love and possibility or a past that's offered you nothing.

"You close yourself off and avoid attachments because of your past, yet here you are with me. Do you want to know why?" he asked. She didn't respond. "The reason is you run and no one follows. No one comes to get you. So you just keep running. You ran away last night, the difference is I followed."

She waited a moment before speaking. "That's pretty good," she finally said after swallowing hard, her voice thick with emotion as she found herself steeped in thoughts she had long since tucked away. "You should have gone into psychoanalysis. You would have been a great shrink."

"Nah, too many crazies out there," he joked, realizing that she was again blocking her feelings from him.

"That's not the real reason."

"No?" he questioned.

"No, the real reason is that you're afraid."

He burst out laughing, almost to tears. "Me, afraid? Okay, I'll bite, what am I afraid of?"

"Of being found out." The joyful levity in his eyes remained consistent. "You run and hide, just like I do. But as I go from place to place avoiding attachments, you hide in plain sight using your psychology degrees as a guise to keep everyone at arm's length. You're the PR director of a huge energy company. You're in the spotlight one hundred percent of the time, yet you remain invisible. I find that curious. I did some research on you last night after dinner."

"I thought this bio was about my grandfather."

"It is. It's also about the Buchanan family, centering on your grandfather's point of view since he connects the past and the present."

"What did you find out about me?"

"Nothing at first. Apparently you're very good at being invisible."

"I'm PR, my job is to put the chairman, CEO and company in the spotlight, not myself. I step into the light only when necessary. So tell me, what else?"

"I dug deeper and found out that you were married a year ago, and then mysteriously you weren't. That was right about the time the company was hit with the hostile takeover bid. My guess is that one had something to do with the other since your ex-wife's family played a sizable role in that takeover strategy. From then on there's been nothing in the public domain about you personally. I wonder why?" He didn't respond. "Funny isn't it, we're more alike then you thought."

He smiled, but said nothing as he looked down at the perfect distraction. "This is Patsy Ann, our very own old faithful. She's an English pit bull terrier and the official city of Juneau greeter."

Jo smiled, leaned down to the statue and touched its head. "Aw, she's adorable," she said. "So tell me, what's the story behind Patsy Ann?"

"Patsy Ann was deaf from birth, but still she somehow heard ship's whistles before they approached. She was never wrong. She'd trot to the wharf to meet them. When she headed to the docks everyone in town would follow knowing there'd be a ship approaching soon even if they didn't see it. They knew to trust Patsy Ann."

Just then a small group of school-age kids ran up and began laughing and playing with the statue. They used sign language to communicate with each other. Jo signed to them. They engaged with her instantly. Turning from side to side, she laughed and signed to them with ease. Andre stepped back and observed the interaction with surprise, then smiled broadly. He was amused at seeing her animated expression as each young teen tried to get and keep her attention.

At one point she signed and the students turned to look at him. It was obvious the current discussion was about him. One of the girls circled her face then brushed her hands together. Another pressed two fingers to her lips then drew her fist to her chest. Some of the other young girls laughed and repeated the two actions. Andre looked at her curiously.

"I think you have the beginning of a fan club here," she said, as well as signed.

"Do I?" he said. She nodded, signing his answer for the others.

There was more signing as the girls giggled and turned to him shyly. "They think you're handsome and want to know if you're my boyfriend." She signed something to them and they all cheered. She didn't translate for him. She glanced up at him then smiled and laughed readily. It was a touching, revealing sight. She obviously connected with children. He wondered what their children might be like.

The stray thought stopped him cold. He realized that he was beginning to feel too much too soon for Jo. He needed to step back and clear his head—fast. The idea was for her to open up to him, not the other way around.

Jo looked around for him again. When she spotted him he nodded and motioned that he would be going into the nearby store. She nodded and went back to chatting with the children and now their teacher. The kids surrounded her laughing and signing.

Andre glanced back before entering the store. He needed to distance himself physically and mentally. This distracting dalliance ploy of his was beginning to backfire. His intent was to get and keep *her* emotionally off balance, not him. Truth be told, emotion wasn't a bad thing, it just wasn't his thing.

He'd successfully removed emotion from the relationship equation. When it came to women they gave him pleasure and he reciprocated, but on his terms. And his terms were to never allow himself to become emotional or feel anything more than necessary. He reminded himself that this was a strictly physical arrangement. If he could dominate her body, then she would lose control over her emotions. And once her heart betrayed her, she'd have to leave.

Andre walked around inside the store a few moments, casually glancing at the jeweled trinkets. A salesperson asked if he needed assistance. He noticed a diamond bracelet in one of the glass cases. It looked perfect for Jo and just what he needed to seal this deal. But before making the purchase he noticed a snow globe in another case. It hit him that the diamond bracelet would work on most women, but he needed something different for Jo. He made a purchase, satisfied that he was back in control.

By the time he exited the store, the children were gone

and Jo was sitting on a bench talking with someone else, a man. Tall, tanned and blond, he had the look of player out to play. He said something. Jo tossed her head back laughing happily. An instant hot streak of jealousy shot through him as a muscle pulled tight in his jaw and a slow strained smile touched his lips.

Andre walked over casually, with a fierce gleam of possessiveness in his eyes. The man looked up and watched him approach. He smiled and leaned in to Jo to say something. She laughed again. He handed her something, she nodded. He shot one last glance at Andre then quickly stood and walked away.

"Making new friends?" Andre asked as he watched the man disappear into the surrounding crowd.

"Of course," she said standing, "I have a thing for kids. I just can't say no. Believe it or not I wanted to be a teacher at one time."

He was referring to the man, but accepted that she spoke about the kids. "Really? Do you have any children of your own?"

"No," she said wistfully, her face sad and joyful at the same time. He walked to stand by her side. She looked around as if it was the last time. "This city is so remarkable and completely impractical."

"Impractical?"

"Totally impractical. It's almost teetering on the side of a mountain. How is that possible? Why would they build a city here? It makes no sense."

"Actually, that would be two mountains."

"I stand corrected, still it's crazy."

"Juneau, the city, was built by miners in the throngs of the Klondike gold rush. I don't think they stopped to assess the land and survey other possible locations. The strategy was simple—find gold, get rich and try not to die."

"I guess you have a good point there. It must have been rough in those times, barely livable by our standards. I wonder how they survived and thrived all those years? I wonder how your great-grandfather did it?"

Taken off guard, Andre turned quickly and stared at her, wondering just how much she really knew about his family. Her expression was placid and gave nothing away.

She saw the questioning expression and it made her wonder. Apparently the cool, reserved and forever cautious Andre Buchanan had been surprised. By what, she couldn't even imagine. "Thank you for today. I got a lot of information that will add depth to the biography. I think Jacob will be delighted."

"Glad to be of service. It's getting late, we should get back. I have some things to take care of and I'm sure you want to get some work done before it gets too late."

She nodded as they headed back to his car. They got in and drove toward Douglas Island. The drive back to the cabin was nearly silent with only occasional conversation. Jo didn't mind so much. She was tired and she figured Andre was too. After all he didn't get nearly as much sleep as she did. Maybe that's why he wasn't in the mood to talk. It was okay with her. She was exhausted keeping her guard up all day. She laid her head back against the headrest and mulled over ideas related to the book.

Andre glanced over and saw her relax against the seat. She looked stunning in the fiery sunlight. He wondered just how close he came to the truth in his assessment of her, because he knew that she was dead-on when it came to her assessment of him.

Chapter 9

It was nearing sunset when they got back. As soon as they arrived they each went their separate ways with plans to meet up for a late dinner. Andre watched as Jo quickly hurried up the stairs intent on working. When he heard the door close, he headed to his grandfather's office to check in.

He'd canceled his busy schedule for the next few days. Taking care of his grandfather's project was infinitely more important. He seldom turned off his BlackBerry, but today he needed to focus and that meant no interruptions of any kind. He had missed four meetings, two conference calls, a magazine interview and the company press briefing. His staff was more than proficient and he knew they'd handle any situation flawlessly. He also knew that he'd receive a full report.

His grandfather had insisted that he clear his schedule, but he refused to just stop everything. As expected, he received a full report on the meetings and conference calls.

He proofed the magazine interview and press briefing, making edits and changes then e-mailing them back. His staff was used to his absence and worked diligently. Still this was his family and his responsibility. He took both seriously. As such, he managed his division with expert precision and a work ethic that was unmatched.

As soon as he walked into the office he turned on his cell and immediately received a message. It was from his assistant with word that a sealed dossier had been sent to him. Seeing it, he picked it up from the desk and opened it. He assumed there would be no surprises, but still he flipped through with a critical eye. As expected, his team delivered expertly.

He called and spoke with his secretaries and assistants catching up on the day's events. As stipulated by him, everything had been handled to his specifications or rescheduled for his personal attention. Afterward he sat at the desk and scanned a barrage of computer e-mails and phone messages received throughout the day. Nothing was particularly earth shattering, so he tabled most. Still others needed his immediate attention. He picked up the phone and went to work.

Three hours later, the day ended with a conference call with his father, brothers and uncle. They brought him up to speed on what had developed in the meeting earlier that day. The prospects were positive and it seemed that everyone was on board.

"We don't anticipate any major obstructions. The briefing was thorough and the principals were extremely impressed."

"So it's a go," he said.

"Not necessarily a go, but extremely positive. Your drafts were very impressive. I think they might just go for it."

"Excellent," Andre said with relief, pleased that his idea

would possibly see fruition. "Is everything ready for the next stage?"

"Affirmative," his brother Quinton answered. "We're headed out to Prudhoe Bay first thing tomorrow."

Andre only half listened after that as his father and brother continued talking about their plans. The idea of re-constructing Titan Energy for the future was a massive undertaking. This critical stage would leave the company exposed to possible takeover attempts. But if their plan worked, they'd be through the vulnerable stage before anyone even got wind of their plans.

By the standards of the mega oil companies in the country, Titan Energy was small but extremely profitable. No one could deny their persistence or reputation. Through the years, big companies had tried to buy or even force them out, but they survived. Adapt and change was the key. There were no longer easy access fields available. All re-maining fields were too hard and too expensive to get to either for geographic or political reasons. Oil was no longer the future fuel source. Titan Energy realized that fact well over a decade ago and had been preparing ever since with biodiesel, wind technology and alternate sources. They were about to announce the company's new direction leading the way to green energy, a division that had already begun gaining prominent status and recognition in the industry.

"Any indication this writer might be looking for more than to write dad's bio?" his uncle asked.

"No, not at this point," Andre said, "but I haven't ruled anything out."

"Need I remind you of the precarious position we find ourselves in at this juncture? This can't get out."

"I agree." Andre didn't need his family to remind him of his duty and obligation. He knew what he had to do. This was too important. Jo was a possible threat to his family and the future of the Buchanan name. He needed to neutralize her without upsetting or drawing attention to either the company or his grandfather.

"So what have you decided to do to get rid of her?"

"I have a few promising ideas," he said, slightly distracted now as his thoughts instantly turned to Jo. He looked up at the ceiling and smiled, wondering what she was doing. An instant later his body reacted to his wayward thoughts.

"Good, keep me posted. I want this wrapped up as soon as possible."

"What's the plan?" his uncle asked.

"Plausible deniability," Andre said, then heard his father and brothers chuckle. "Just know that I'm taking care of it."

"Cautiously I hope, your grandfather is no fool. You need to move with deliberate haste and vigilance."

"I understand," Andre said, knowing that he would tread the narrow line he drew between himself and Jo. He was gaining her trust and opening her heart to him. He just needed a little more time to seal the deal. Once she admitted her feelings for him and her obvious conflict of interest in writing this bio, she'd have no choice but to leave. "It's being handled," he assured his family. The conference call ended.

Andre immediately turned his attention back to work only to realize that his mind was no longer focused on the job. He looked up at the ceiling and considered the day he spent with Jo. He was surprised how easy it was to get to know her. Perhaps he was wrong. Maybe she had no ulterior motive, but he couldn't take that chance. This was too important to all concerned.

If she was as she appeared, and his plan progressed, then he'd deal with that if and when it happened. On the other hand, if indeed her intentions were more dubious, then she would deserve exactly what he intended to do, and her reputation would be irreparably damaged. He would do everything within his power to make sure of it. Either way he needed to be cautious.

He picked up a pen and twirled it between his fingers imagining all the things he would do. A slow seductive smile formed on his lips. Thinking of her, as he found himself doing more and more, prompted his body to react again. He wanted her. But that was nothing unusual. He had wanted her all day long. Even now, just thinking about the possibilities increased his pulse rate and hardened his desire.

He thought about Jo's interaction with the kids at the Patsy Ann statue. There was something about the way she joked and played with them then stood back laughing that touched him. He remembered the feeling of pleasure and pride in knowing that she was with him. The stray feeling of belonging warmed him.

Seconds later his smile slowly faded when his thoughts wandered again to the man talking to her. He'd never been jealous of anyone a single day in his life. It wasn't in his nature, yet the feelings were unmistakable. He felt his detachment threatened, he wasn't supposed to feel anything, least of all jealousy.

He needed to clear his mind. The whole idea was for him to affect her, not the other way around. He glanced up at the ceiling again then got up and went into the kitchen. Cooking dinner would be his distraction.

Jo had gone directly to her bedroom. As soon as she walked in she felt the blast of chilly air. But right now she needed chilly after spending the afternoon with Andre. She crossed the room and sat on the bed sighing heavily. She was exhausted, but deliriously happy. The day had been close to perfect. Andre was a fun tour guide and she was sure he was beginning to open up and trust her. Satisfied, she kicked off her boots and looked around.

All of the sudden it was obvious that someone had been there. She'd made the bed earlier, but now saw that the sheets had been changed and the bed remade to four-star hotel perfection including mints in a dish on the nightstand beside the bottled water. She got up and continued looking around. There were fresh towels in the bathroom and her discarded clothes had been cleaned and left neatly folded on the stand by the wardrobe.

She put the clothes away, changed back into her red cashmere sweater and slacks from earlier then walked over to the office area and looked at the desk. Everything was exactly as she left it except that a new printer had been set up and placed on the side desk with available connections to her laptop at the ready. She sat amazed by the proficiency of the Buchanan household, then attached the printer and turned on her laptop.

Before actually writing again, she opened and reviewed the boxes she'd gone through that morning and the day before. She had divided the information into several piles. Today she intended to focus on the Buchanans' early years, before Jacob. She turned to her laptop and reviewed the outline she'd begun earlier. The overall tone was good, but for some reason the piece still seemed stiff and rigid. It didn't feel like the open and easy exchange of information with a man like Jacob.

She sat thinking for a few moments, toying with new directions. Her many phone interviews and conversations with Jacob showed him to be a gracious man who valued hard work and loved his family. Andre was a lot like that as well. She considered her day with Andre and realized that, age and position aside, he and Jacob were very much alike.

They were intelligent, honest, forthright men who worked hard and were solely and completely dedicated to the family business. She started reworking the opening of the bio incorporating information from her many pages of notes, from conversations with Jacob and details from the boxes.

The result was far better than she expected. The direction was comfortable and easy while expressing the hardships of a century past. She attached the headphones to her computer and began replaying the recorded interviews and conversations she had had with Jacob the last few weeks.

Suddenly Jo had a rush of inspiration. She typed nonstop for the next few hours, narrowing and revising her manuscript while continuing her research. When she finally took a break she noticed that the room was not only dark but cold again. She drank a bottle of water then continued writing. An hour later she stopped, saving her file to the laptop hard drive and two flash drives.

She got up, stretched and walked to the window. Shivering, she realized just how cold the bedroom had gotten. It was completely dark outside. She'd worked through the entire evening. "Maybe I shouldn't have mentioned his great-grandfather," she muttered, second-guessing herself about their conversation earlier that day. The thought popped into her head and seemed to come from nowhere. Maybe she was wrong about him, considering everything that happened that day. The morning ride up the mountain and the walking tour in town both revealed Andre as open and welcoming.

Ten minutes later Jo was still staring out the window when she smelled something incredible. Her stomach growled instantly. She realized she was hungry and whatever was cooking downstairs smelled delicious.

Following the heavenly aroma, she went into the kitchen just as a blast of smoke puffed up over the range.

Andre stood at the grill basting salmon fillets with what
looked like an herb butter mixture. Still attired in the jeans
and shirt from earlier, he'd added a cook's apron. She
watched awhile, noting for the first time just how sexy it
was to watch a man cooking. He was fully engaged in his
task, moving with agility and aptness. "Hey," she said
from the doorway, after taking her time watching him.

Andre turned at the sound of her voice. She'd changed
back into the outfit she had on earlier that morning. She
looked just as sexy as if she'd worn a negligee. "Hey
yourself," he said smiling.

"I thought you mentioned something about eating
dinner out this morning."

"Call me selfish, I thought we'd spend the evening
here."

Jo bit at her lower lip not knowing how to reply to a
remark like that. "Need some help?"

"Sure, grab the oven mitts and pull the potatoes out of
the oven. They should be done."

She did as he instructed. She opened the oven expecting to see two baked potatoes, but instead pulled out a tray
of crispy glazed sweet potatoes. The aroma was mouth-
watering. Her stomach growled again, tempting her to pop
one into her mouth, but she didn't. "Wow, these look incredible," she said placing the tray on a trivet.

"Try one," he said, grabbing a small slice and offering
it to her. She touched his hand as he guided the hot potato
to her mouth. She bit it in half. It was hot, but the taste was
pure heavenly decadence.

"That's delicious," she said as he popped the rest of the
potato into his mouth and then turned his focus back to the
salmon. Grabbing his tongs, he turned the salmon to cross-
hatch the grill marks. "Here, you can put the potatoes on
this plate. Careful, it's warm."

She grabbed the heated serving plate with the mitts and began piling the potatoes on top. "Done," she said. He reached over, grabbed the plate and placed the salmon fillets alongside the potatoes. He sprinkled chopped parsley on top then put the plate on the counter already set with two place settings. She followed him to the counter. "Wow, this looks and smells amazing."

"Have a seat," he said, pulling the stool out for her.

She sat down and waited as he grabbed a bottle of wine, opened it and filled both their glasses. "You really are full of surprises," she said.

"Is that good?" he asked, holding his glass up to her.

She picked up her glass and gently touched it to his. "Yes, it's very good." They each took a sip of wine, and then she looked at the meal in front of her. Everything looked sensational. Andre served both plates then sipped his wine waiting for her to try the food. She tasted the salmon and baby vegetables then sliced a portion of sweet potato. The taste exploded in her mouth in an array of flavors and textures. It was sweet, savory and crisp. "This is fantastic. Who taught you how to cook?" she asked, dabbing at her mouth.

"Confession time—I can only cook four different meals."

"What are the other three?" she asked.

"I think I'll wait and surprise you," he teased. They continued eating while chatting about the day spent in Juneau. When they finished, they sat sipping wine and eased into various topics of conversation. "So tell me, what was your number one favorite part about our tour today?" he asked.

"All of it."

"Uh-uh, that's a cop-out. You have to name one thing."

"Okay, one thing," she pondered a moment. "All right, I

have it. I'd say my number one favorite part of today was seeing the view from the top of the mountain this morning. I still can't believe how amazing it was. The idea that it's yours and you can go up there anytime you want is awesome."

"It's a very special place. I have a lot of great memories there. I'm glad you liked being there. Perhaps we can go up there again before you leave," he said, as he gathered the dishes and placed them in the dishwasher.

"I'd like that," she said, smiling while helping him load dishes. She chuckled softly as she handed him the silverware.

He looked over and noticed her expression. "What?" he asked.

"Nothing."

"No, for real, what is it?"

"I was just thinking that I might have been wrong about you before."

"Oh really, what exactly did you think about me before?"

"Basically that you were a spoiled, arrogant, self-serving, playboy millionaire snob," she rattled off instantly. Andre laughed out loud and continued laughing. "That wasn't exactly a compliment you know," she added.

"I know, but I still love it. Believe it or not it's not the first time I've heard myself described like that, although the self-serving part is a nice added touch. So tell me, what do you think of me now?"

"Did I forget to mention conceited?" she joked.

"Conceited? No. Interested in your opinion, definitely."

"Okay, I guess charming would be a good description."

"Charming," he repeated while nodding approvingly, "I like that. I can do charming." He started the dishwasher and walked toward the doorway where she stood.

"Will you answer a personal question?" she began.

"If you have a drink with me first," he said. "Come on, I have something special I think you'll enjoy trying."

She followed him to the library and stood as he placed a pitcher of ice water and two crystal glasses on the bar then placed a slotted spoon over each glass. He dropped one sugar cube onto each spoon then poured green liquid from a stylized black bottle with green eyes. She watched intently, impressed by the extreme production. The aroma of licorice filled the air. "What are you doing, what is all this?"

"You'll see," he said, continuing to mix the concoction. He took a lighter and set the sugar cube on fire. Instantly a blue blaze appeared and burned through the sugar.

Jo picked up the black bottle with its eerie green eyes and read the name. "Absinthe Superieure," she looked up at him. "Isn't absinthe illegal in the United States?"

"No, not anymore," he said, as the fire died down and he added ice water from the pitcher. The drink turned a milky white color. He removed the spoons and handed her a glass. "For you," he said. "Careful, it's strong, but trust me, no little green fairies or other hallucinations, I promise."

She took the glass and held it up, looking at it closely. "I can't believe I'm doing this." She took a small sip. The taste was a mixture of anise and sweet peppermint. She was just savoring it on her palate when her throat began to burn. She gasped from the 124 proof backdraft. When she finally caught her breath she smiled. "Actually that's not too bad."

He smiled, impressed by her adventurous spirit. "Good, I'm glad you tried it. So what's the question?"

She took another small sip. "You were married such a short time, who broke it off?"

"I did," he said plainly. "It lasted two weeks."

"Two weeks," she repeated.

"Do you want to know why?" he asked.

"Do you want to tell me why?" she asked, hoping he would.

"I will, later. But right now, this is for you," he said, as he placed a box on the bar in front of her.

"For me?" she questioned, looking at the box oddly. "I told you, I don't take bribes," she joked.

"Good, because I don't give bribes. Here take it. It won't bite, I promise," he said smiling.

Jo took the box, removed the lid and pulled out a tissue-covered snow globe. She smiled. "Oh, it's beautiful." She turned it upside down, shook it gently and then watched the delicate crystals gently fall back in place. She laughed softly. "Thank you, this was very sweet of you."

"I'm glad you like it," he said as he came from behind the bar and stood in front of her. He reached up and touched her lips softly. "I find that I enjoy pleasing you."

She held her breath and nearly melted on the spot. If this was a dream she never wanted to wake up. But she knew it wasn't and she knew she couldn't go down that road with him. "Andre, why are you doing this?"

"Because I like you," he said softly, then leaned in and kissed her cheek and nuzzled her neck seductively. "I'm beginning to like you way too much," he whispered in her ear.

Her stomach lurched and chills shot through her, making her shudder. The absinthe effect was nothing compared to this man. "You don't even know me."

He stopped and leaned back looking into her eyes. "You don't trust me do you?" he asked.

"I don't know who to trust, the man who vowed to get rid of me or the man who made me dinner tonight."

"There's another choice," he offered. She looked up at him with questioning eyes. "The man who wants to make love to you." She opened her mouth to reply and he kissed her. His tongue slipped easily into her mouth and she savored the feel of being connected to him again. Absinthe to absinthe, the fire between them ignited all over again. Suddenly there was no thought or reason, no discussion or debate. There was only a man and a woman wanting to be in each other's arms.

Jo melted against his body, feeling desire drain her logic away. He encircled her waist, drawing her close. She felt the hardness of his desire press into her. She closed her eyes as her heart pounded like a jackhammer. When the kiss ended she held her hand out and stepped away, shaking her head. "I don't think this is a good idea. It has disaster written all over it. I can't do this," she said breathlessly.

"I was hoping we'd do something different," he tempted.

She closed her eyes trying to find strength. "Andre."

"Sh," he whispered, "I just want you to know that I really like you. I really like you way too much and that wasn't part of the plan," he said, more truthful than he expected.

"Andre," Jo sighed.

"Sit, relax, finish your drink. Tomorrow we'll see Juneau's more touristy sights. It'll probably take up most of the morning and afternoon. We'll hit the gold mine, the glaciers, the museums, and the cemetery and then grab the Mount Roberts tramway to the top. The view is spectacular. I suggest we leave early, it'll be a full day, so until then, pleasant dreams." He backed up and walked away.

Jo stood staring after him, not sure what had just happened. But whatever it was she definitely needed a cold shower to get her through the night. She wasn't sure if it was the absinthe or the fire Andre set burning all through her body, but she definitely needed to chill. She waited a few minutes then went upstairs to her room.

Chapter 10

What had been chilly and cold was now freezing.

She turned and knocked on Andre's bedroom door. He answered almost instantly. She almost forgot what she was going to ask him. "Is it always supposed to be so cold in my bedroom? I was working earlier and suddenly realized that it was freezing. It's even colder now. My teeth are beginning to chatter."

"Each room has a separate thermostat. Housekeeping usually sets the level. I can…" he began, and then looked behind her into the room "…turn your heat up, if you like."

"Oh yes, that would be great. I appreciate it," Jo said, then stepped aside and followed him across the hall back into her bedroom. She watched as he walked over to the office area and adjusted a small thermostat on the wall that she hadn't even noticed before. "There you go, that should do it," he said, then turned to her. His eyes hit two distinct points beneath her sweater. Her nipples were hard. His body instantly reacted.

"Thanks, it's so cold," she said, knowing exactly what drew his attention. She turned away and walked back to the open door.

"You get used to it after awhile," he said as he followed.

"Um, about what happened downstairs between us, I think it might be best if we avoid situations like that from now on. It would complicate my job here."

"Complicate *your* job, you're kidding right?" he joked.

She smiled and chuckled. "I stand corrected, it complicates *both* our jobs. So maybe we can…"

"…call a truce?" he offered, with his hand extended.

She looked at his hand, doubting his sincerity. "Do you even know what a truce is?"

"Ouch, that almost hurt," he said. "Come on, a truce?"

"Fine," she nodded and shook his hand. "Agreed," she said softly. He didn't release her hand. She looked up into his eyes. "Don't," she said.

"Don't what?" he asked innocently.

"You know what, look at me like that."

"Like what?" he asked innocently.

"Now look who's playing games."

"You're right," he said smiling, releasing her hand. "Cards on the table?" he asked. She nodded. "What happened at the airport, and today in Juneau, I enjoyed it."

"I did too, Cannon," she said then chuckled, "Oh, I get it, Cannon as in Buchanan, right?"

"That's one meaning," he said, smiling with that same gleam in his eyes.

She understood his implication instantly. "You're doing it again."

"I can't help it," he said as his broad smile suddenly faded into seriousness. "I'm attracted to you. You already know that. You're attracted to me as well…" She opened her mouth to protest, but found she had nothing to say when he cut her off, "…that is if we're being honest with ourselves."

"Honest or not, some attractions can be dangerous. They can get people in trouble and they can get people hurt," she said.

"And you know this how?" he asked, curious about her experiences.

"My foster parents were attracted to each other. But they were toxic, their so-called attraction hurt everybody around them. I never want to be like that. I remember they'd have affairs all the time and to reconcile with each other they'd fabricate something and blame it on the foster kids, like their drama was our fault. It was a vicious cycle. They'd argue and fight, then attack and blame us."

"That was wrong, they were wrong, but you can't live based on one bad experience. Attractions are a natural human reaction to physical, emotional or other carnal appetites. They manifest in sensual desires. It's false expectations that get people in trouble. State parameters up front and don't go beyond that point."

"That's all well and good, but people and particularly emotions don't stay within a certain set of parameters. It's not in our nature," she said, wondering where this was leading.

He smiled as if he expected her to come to that conclusion. "You do, I do. It's in *our* personal nature to not get attached."

"Yeah, so?" she wondered aloud.

"I have a suggestion, a proposal if you will."

"I'm listening," she said curiously.

"We set parameters and relinquish our reservations for one night. We enjoy each other's bodies and then go back to our respective corners at dawn."

Jo tried to look disinterested, but failed miserably. "In other words, displaced sexual frustration, a one-night stand," she confirmed. He nodded. "No ties."

"No strings," he added.

"No commitments," she said.

"Pure mutual pleasure," he replied.

"A physical release," she said.

"Just sex," he clarified explicitly.

"Just sex," she repeated, and then slowly walked away considering his suggestion. The idea had merit, but it was also fraught with danger. What if what happened the last time happened again? "I can't do it," she said quickly, forcing herself from temptation. "It's unprofessional and there are too many obvious complications."

"Such as you falling in love with me, becoming obsessed? Yeah, I see your point," he joked, easing the tension.

She smiled and laughed. "I guess I forgot to add arrogant in my assessment of you. But seriously, I just," she paused not wanting to go into her past. "Trust me, it would be complicated in the end."

"One night, no strings, no complications, just pure physical pleasure," he tempted.

She turned and walked away. It had obviously been too long for her since she was actually considering his proposal. It was wrong on so many different levels. They'd known each other for just a few days. He was her client's grandson. Sexual attraction or not, how could she just fall into bed with him? Everything inside of her brain screamed stop, but she couldn't help herself. Her body and her heart screamed the loudest.

Still, the question was his parameters. She knew she'd keep them in place, she was concerned about him. Then she considered what she knew about his character. By all accounts he was cold, calculating and generally unemotional. She smiled and turned back to him. If she thought more she knew she wouldn't do it. "Okay, say we do this, how exactly would it work?"

He smiled. "Simple, come here," he said seductively as he turned and closed the bedroom door. She walked over to stand right in front of him. He pulled her close against his body and felt her tense. Then he leaned in and kissed her forehead chastely as he ran his hands up her back over the soft, smooth cashmere. He began massaging her shoulders. "Relax," he whispered.

"I've never done anything like this before. I guess you do this all the time," she said, suddenly nervous.

"No," he said simply, "just this time." She looked up at him cautiously. He was sincere. "Nothing will happen that you don't want to happen. Trust me. Close your eyes, relax," he cooed.

She did and instantly began to relax as the massage continued. "Mmm, that feels good."

"This is nice," he said of her sweater.

"Thanks, it's my favorite. I like the feel of cashmere on my bare skin."

He rubbed his hands down the front of the sweater and smiled as he teased her nipples to harden even more. Her nerve endings clinched and tingled, causing her to gasp and shudder. Apparently delighted with her reaction, he continued touching the soft wool as he dipped his mouth to her neck. "I think after tonight, I will too," he whispered close to her ear. He reached up and touched her lips tenderly. "Do you have any idea how much I want you right now?"

Brazen boldness, stoked by a hot fire of desire burned through her body. She looked down and touched the front of his jeans. His protruding erection was very evident. "I think I have a pretty good idea," she said seductively.

He stood motionless as she reached up and began un-buttoning his shirt. Each button seemed to give her more and more confidence. When she was done she pulled the shirttails from his jeans. She opened the shirt, pushing it back over his shoulders and letting it fall to the carpet. His chest was broad and sweet chocolaty smooth. She ran her hands over him feeling the power and strength of each muscle. Carved like a granite sculpture, she could tell he worked out. A body like his didn't just happen by chance. She leaned in and kissed him, satisfying her chocolate craving. He wasn't chocolate, but he was just as sweet.

He didn't move, just stood stoic and allowed her to play. She played. Kissing and caressing, she kneaded his chest, feeling the firm tightness. He was completely solid. She kissed his nipples gently then felt his body twitch and his stomach quiver. She steadied her focus on making him shudder and to her delight, he did each time she relished his body.

Then with boldness and little hesitation, she began to unbuckle his belt. He still didn't move so she continued. She unfastened his jeans button. The back of her hand brushed against his arousal. Biting her lower lip, she slowly unzipped his jeans and she ran her finger under his waistband then eagerly slipped her hand inside. The treasure she found nearly floored her. She shuddered inside anticipating the next few moments. She attempted to dip inside again, but was stopped when he took her hands and held them still. She looked up at him. He smiled. "My turn."

His voice was deep and menacing, causing her to wonder just what she'd agreed to. After all there were no set rules to this night of pure pleasure. The idea of him tying her to the bed popped into her head. She shuddered, not because she feared the act, but because perhaps she wanted it. He had a way of looking at her that seemed to weaken her and made her want to break her will. It was a power struggle with winner taking all.

With her hand still in his, he led her to the bed then turned and sat, positioning her close between his long legs. She stood looking down at him wondering what he had in mind. She soon found out. He unbuttoned and unzipped her pants, pulled and helped them fall to the plush carpet. Then he raised the bottom edge of her cashmere sweater up over her head. She stood now wearing only black lace panties. The result left him speechless. He looked up and down the length of her body with slow deliberate enjoyment. Afterward he just stared straight ahead motionlessly, readily feasting his eyes on two perfectly rounded orbs.

Her heart was beating furiously and the parts of her inside that hadn't already gelled burned like lava. She wasn't sure if he liked what he saw. Suddenly self-conscious, Jo covered her breasts with her hands. It seemed to somehow break his trance. He looked up at her as he moved her hands to her sides. "Don't ever cover these from me," he said sincerely.

He opened his mouth again, but didn't speak this time. Instead, he drew her close and touched his tongue lightly to her pebbled nipple. A quick tickling sensation shot through her like white lightning. She quivered and tried to jerk away, but he held too firm and looked up. "Jo, did I hurt you?"

She licked her dried lips and shook her head. "No."

He smiled satisfied, then repeated the action. She shuddered again. The madness of his mouth caused all kinds of smoldering fires to ignite inside of her. Lava flowed though her veins. Now, instead of just licking her, he'd whole-heartedly devoured her breasts each in turn and then pushed them together to consume them in unison. His mouth was hot and her body, once chilled, was now on fire. The result was a mindless inferno of passion.

His hands came around to encircle her waist. She held tight to his shoulders giving him everything he wanted. Her head tossed back, she nearly screamed from the sheer vigor of his onslaught. Then he reached up, placed his hand behind her neck and brought her to his mouth. He kissed her with a raging passion, seeming intent on shattering her mind. His masterful wayward hands crept between her legs and stroked her there. Her body began gyrating rhythmically to his hand movements. Her legs trembled, weakened then buckled. She collapsed onto his lap, spreading her legs, straddling him as he sat. The kiss continued. His tongue danced in her mouth as he held her rear, pressing her even closer to his stone hard erection.

Her thoughts hazed and her body took over. She was feeling everything, his hands, his mouth, his tongue, his chest. Thinking rationally was out of the question. Then from a wayward corner in the back of her mind it hit her. She leaned back. "Wait, wait, condoms, I don't have any," she rasped breathlessly.

His breath was just as ragged. "Drawer, bottom, nightstand, by the bed." Understanding, she slid off his lap and moved to the nightstand. She bent over and opened the drawer finding notepaper, pens, a calculator and hand lotion. Then she finally found a box of condoms. She opened it and grabbed one, pulling the four also attached.

Andre had watched as she leaned over to open the drawer. The apple bottom he'd fixated on before dinner dried his mouth instantly. He stood up and quickly removed his pants and shorts. When she turned back to him, he stood naked. She smiled looking down the length of him. He was magnificent. Then she focused on his erection. A quick shiver swept through her as she felt her body go wet. He was thick and long and just what she needed.

"Come here," he said. She walked back over to him. He turned her around and dropped to his knees facing the apple of his appetite. He smiled and admired its perfection then touched and gently caressed the soft brown cheeks. This was what he wanted. He held her hips, drew her back and licked her cheek then kissed and nibbled her. She took a step away, but he held her tight with no intention of letting go.

Jo closed her eyes, too wracked with desire to do anything else. She was about to explode. No one had ever made her feel so wanted and desired. She stepped away again, this time he released her. She turned and looked down as he looked up. Their eyes stayed connected while he took the condoms still in her hand, tore one open and protected them. He stood and wrapped his arms around her waist and drew her close. The sudden action made her gasp. Her mouth open, he leaned down and kissed her passionately. Demanding and possessively, he seared his mouth to hers.

She consciously knew that he'd picked her up, but she had no idea what took so long to get to the bed. He carried her then finally laid her down with her head on the pillow and captured her lips once more. Long and lasting, the kiss faded to nibbles across her face, down her neck, down her chest, across her breasts, to her stomach.

Her arousal was more than complete as her body's fluid poured out to welcome him. If he went lower she was sure she'd burst into a million pieces. He did, French kissing her there. "Andre, now," she demanded. He ignored her; he was too busy enjoying himself. She shook in spasms ready to explode. She grabbed at his shoulder. "Andre, please come inside."

He leaned up and moved her leg aside, and then lay

down on top of her. He looked down between them and smiled. She wrapped her legs around his waist feeling the pressure of his erection at her core. In one smooth motion they each pressed, uniting their bodies. His fullness plunged deep, all the way inside of her. She gasped aloud then whimpered and dug her nails into his back. The exquisite pleasure and pain nearly brought her to tears. Deep inside of her he remained still and looked down at her. "Are you okay?" Her tightness surprised him. She wasn't a virgin, he knew that much, but she was extremely tight.

Breathless from the pleasure, she nodded, "Yes, it's just been awhile."

"Do you want me to stop?" he asked. She shook her head. "Do you want me to go slow?" She smiled and shook her head again. She wanted this too much, she wanted him too much. She lifted her hips upward, grinding into him.

With deliberate ease he began to move inside of her, slowly at first then soon with more vigor and power. Surging in and out, he plunged deeper and deeper over and over again. She met each plunge with one of her own positioning herself just right. His body stroked her with each move. The building climax could not be held back. She screamed seconds before he covered her mouth with his as he also reached his climax.

His body trembled and shook as a wave drained him. When he went still, she moved her hips and he shook again. "Don't move," he said. His eyes were closed, his head was arched back and his mouth was open. His breathing was more like panting. She smiled, having wreaked havoc on his body in such a way. She moved her hips again. He groaned and tried to move away from her. He rolled to the side. She rolled with him, landing on top. He looked up at her, surprised by the action. She smiled and sat back on his hips comfortably. "You're not going anywhere, it's not dawn yet. More," she said playfully.

He instantly cupped her breasts and smiled, ready to give her exactly what she asked for, although to his pleasure and hers, not exactly how she expected.

Chapter 11

Some time later Jo woke up slowly feeling a tingling sensation flood inside her. There was a body pressed behind her, holding her, touching her, making her body burn all over again. She smiled slowly, remembering the last time. The man was full of surprises. Who would have imagined her body could do that twice. "Hey," she said sleepily.

"It's about time you woke up," he whispered, seductively stroking the sensitive curve between her shoulder and hip. She shivered and tried to inch away. He held her tight. "You're not going anywhere, it's not dawn yet," he echoed.

"I think I've created a monster."

"I don't know about a monster, but you definitely brought something to life."

She felt it too. "What are you doing to me back there?" she asked knowingly.

"Whatever you want me to do," he promised with a

whisper as his hand came forward to cup her breast and fondle the nipple, rubbing it between his thumb and forefinger. He moved even closer.

"I'm wondering if that's your knee back there."

"No," he said, while kissing the nape of her neck and then her shoulder as his hand drifted farther down. "Want to guess again?" he asked.

Her nerves tingled and her heart began beating rapidly. His hand dipped between her legs. She gasped. "I think you need to stop doing that," she warned.

"Actually, I'm thinking that I need to do a bit more. Got any ideas, 'cause I do." He rolled onto his back taking her with him. Now she lay on top with her back pressing onto him. "Shame we don't have a mirror. I think I'd like to see this."

She looked up at the ceiling. It looked different than it did earlier. But this wasn't the time to worry about that. "See what?" she asked.

"See this," he whispered as his hands covered her breasts and rubbed her already tightened nipples. She closed her eyes, happy that there was no mirror. She couldn't imagine what else he might do, and then he began to do it. His hand moved down, spreading her legs farther apart. "What are you going to…" Before she finished the question, she felt his fingers spread her open then dip inside of her. She felt her inside muscles contract to close tight around him. Her body trembled as he slipped out then back in again. "Andre," she gasped breathlessly.

"Shh, I need to picture you in my mind's eye when I do this."

"Do what?" she asked, then knew instantly. She trembled and shook when he found and tweaked her swollen nub then began stroking it. Instantly a fierce intense climax began to grow inside. He stroked and prodded her as she poured out for him. He was gentle as each tender touch thrust her closer and closer to the pinnacle of her climax. She felt a spasm coming and tried her best to endure. Seconds later she exploded.

She lay there on top of him trying desperately to catch her breath. He had too many tricks up his sleeve to play fair. She looked up at the unfamiliar ceiling again. "What happened to one time only?"

"This is one time only. I just haven't finished with you and as you so eloquently put it, it's not yet dawn."

"That sounds a lot like double-talk," she said as she rolled off him. She lay on her stomach hoping to deter his ardor, at least for the moment. She had no idea that the plump roundness of her rear made him even harder. "This isn't fair, you cheat."

He lay on his side, stroking her back and rubbing her rear. Playfully he squeezed and massaged her, fascinated by how much he enjoyed looking at and touching her. "True," he said then stopped, "I can always leave." He rolled over to get out of the bed. He sat on the edge knowing that she would stop him. She did, but not as he expected.

Jo sat up, quickly grabbed a condom from the table and moved to the edge of the bed. She sat on her knees behind him pressing her breasts to his back and wrapped her hands around his neck and down his chest. She dipped to his ear. "Are you sure you want to leave?" She tweaked his nipples to make her point. He groaned as his head rolled back. She nipped his neck and felt him shudder and continued stimulating his nipples.

"I think you need to stop doing that," he warned.

"Wasn't that just my line?" she asked, knowing that the heat of her breath in his ear would excite him. In an instant he reached back and pulled her to his lap. She straddled the front of him showing him the condom in her hand.

"Open it," he said.

She did, and then very deliberately she eased it onto him. "Now that you have me here, Mr. Buchanan, what do you have in mind?" she asked.

His eyes burned into hers and suddenly stillness seemed to surround him. There, looking into her eyes, he felt something that he never experienced before. This was more, he wanted more. Andre slowly reached up and touched her lips, seemingly hypnotized by his own actions. His hand scrolled across her jaw and down her neck to her shoulder to finally encircle each pebbled nipple. He smiled and he drew a figure eight from one nipple to the next.

The scant weight of her rounded breasts seemed to fascinate him. He cupped each with his large hand then circled each nipple with his palms, causing her to gasp. He leaned in, opened his mouth and slowly, sensually licked the hardened bud. Her body shuddered and quaked. He kissed and sucked her, pulling her deep into the warmth of his mouth. He continued the torturous ecstasy as his other hand gently massaged and caressed the other breast.

Jo's head rolled back, arching her body forward giving him more access to his ravaged treasure. She held tight to his shoulders as her hips began to search for his erection. She pulled back, sat up and came down quickly, impaling her body onto his hardness. She began to gyrate slow and easy, as if she were riding a mechanical bull in slow motion.

Pulsating in pleasure, he held her waist and watched as her body moved in slow erotic pleasure. She held his neck loosely as her rounded breasts teased his chest. She sat up high, maneuvering her breast just inches away from his mouth. When he opened to take her in, she moved away smiling. He allowed her to continue the teasing, knowing that this was only the beginning.

They watched each other as her motion increased. She moved faster and faster, inching seconds away from her climax. It came and overtook her. She grimaced and muffled a scream. Then surprisingly he stood. Still connected, she held tight as he began to walk. Suddenly her back was pressed against a wall. He kissed her as he began to thrust into her. Her precarious position didn't allow her to reciprocate. Within moments he came, bursting everything he had into her.

She held tight pressed between him and the wall. After a few moments he released her. She slid until her foot touched the soft carpet. Before the other foot came down, he picked her up and took her back to the bed. They lay together wrapped in each other's arms. There were no words. The room was still dark so she closed her eyes to sleep again. What seemed like only moments later she heard him speak one word. "Dawn," he whispered.

"It's almost daybreak already," she said sleepily. "I don't think I slept ten minutes straight all night."

"Regrets already?" he asked.

"Hardly," she said, "I'm just not going to be at my best for work today."

"We'll spend most of the day in Juneau."

"I still have to get my work done or is that the plan." She went still, closed her eyes and shook her head.

"What plan?" he asked.

"Distract me from working?"

"Make love all night, most definitely, a plan to distract you from working, not exactly my style."

She sat up and looked into his eyes. He looked sincere, but she wasn't sure. "How do I trust you?"

He smiled mischievously. "Trust me now."

"And what about when dawn breaks?" she asked, lying back down on his chest. She closed her eyes, smiled and drifted off to sleep once more.

"Dawn's a different story," he said before dozing off himself.

Chapter 12

Tomorrow came too quickly. Andre sat in Jacob's home office working or doing a lousy job of trying to work. It was impossible. In the middle of a conference call with his staff he canceled it for no reason other than his thoughts wandered constantly. All he kept thinking about was Jo upstairs in his bed.

He awoke after dawn and lay watching her sleep. She was perfect. He resisted waking her and making love again. That wasn't the bargain. So all he could do now was savor the memories.

She was adventurous, he'd give her that. She'd accepted his proposal almost immediately. The result was a night of passion that he'd remember for a long while to come. It was a shame it was only one night.

He considered the prospect of more nights with her. The possibilities of what they could do were endless. One in particular made him smile. His thoughts, centered on the fantasy, lasted much longer that he expected. He definitely needed to consider installing a ceiling mirror in one of his bedrooms.

Earlier, while dressing, he mentally reviewed everything they did, reliving the best parts with a broad smile on his face. Actually, they were all the best parts. She was amazing. Playful just enough, sexy just enough and heaven knows brazen just enough. She'd surprised him to say the least. And what was even more surprising was his reaction to her.

Somewhere during the night he found himself breaking his own rule. At one point he looked into her eyes and imagined more. He backed off of course, but it was the idea that he even went there that disturbed him. She had an intoxicating power over him. Maybe it was because she was so different than the women he usually associated with.

They'd chatted at times, argued at others. He smiled and chuckled even now. About football of all things, she was a huge football fan. The season was already in play and they'd each speculated as to what teams would be in the Super Bowl and why. He shook his head in wonderment. She was amazing, too amazing. The smiled faded, just as it did earlier. He still questioned everything. Trust never was his strong suit.

Joanna's senses gradually came to life. She opened her eyes slowly and looked at the window on the opposite wall. Heavy drapes covered the window except of a thin sliver of sunshine beaming through. Not only was it dawn, it was day. She sat up and looked around. The room was different, darker, more masculine. She knew instantly that she was no longer in the guest bedroom.

She got up too quickly and her body objected. She was sore and stiff. Apparently one night with Andre had completely worn her down. She couldn't imagine being with him night after night. Then she smiled and began to wonder what it *would* be like. Having him at her beck and call to do with as she pleased would be any woman's fantasy. He was the total package, sexy, smart and rich. But he wasn't for her. As they'd promised each other, until dawn and that was it.

She gathered the sheet around her body and looked around seeing that apparently he had kept his word. Dawn had come and gone and he was nowhere in sight. She walked to the window and peeked outside. The sight was breathtaking. She was completely enthralled by the splendor. The landscaped, lush greenery of the front lawn was perfectly tended. Flowering shrubs accentuated the curved drive leading to the pristine home raised slightly above the knoll.

Jacob's house stood atop a hill looking down at total beauty. Across was a misty fog, but still showed evidence of a city, she presumed was Juneau. It was a panoramic pictorial of splendor. "You've gotta be kidding me. For real, who lives like this?"

She turned back to the bedroom, obviously Andre's bedroom, and wondered how she got here. As far as she could remember they had been in the same room all night. He'd picked her up, but only twice, once during the first time and once during the last time. She opened the door and peeked out. To her relief her bedroom was directly across the hall.

She looked up and down the hall, held her breath and dashed across to the guest bedroom. Once inside she leaned back against the closed door and exhaled. She quickly rummaged through her suitcases finding wool pants, a thick turtleneck sweater and a fleece-lined windbreaker. She quickly chose her outfit, jumped in the shower and got dressed.

On her way downstairs she considered again what it would be like to make love to Andre every night. The man was insatiable. She definitely wouldn't mind another one-night stand, but she knew she'd be pressing her luck. She didn't want to make the relationship more complicated than it already was.

There was a nice guy somewhere in all that macho swagger and the last thing she wanted to do was to hurt him. So, one night will just have to be enough.

She looked around in the living room, dining room and kitchen. There was a pot of coffee with cups but no one in sight. She opened the sliding door and stepped out on the veranda. The air was chilled and the sky sparkled and just as before, the view was breathtaking. She stood for a moment to clear her thoughts. She needed to put last night behind her and continue what she started. She needed to talk to Andre.

She went back inside and found Andre in Jacob's office. He sat at the huge power desk looking like the *only bad boy*. She couldn't help but want him all over again. There wasn't a woman alive who probably didn't. But wanting another night in his bed was way too much to consider, even for her. "Good morning," she said.

Andre looked up and saw Jo standing in the doorway to the office. He leaned back in his chair, smiling automatically. "Good morning, barely," he nodded at the wall clock, seeing that it was closer to noon.

"Yeah, I guess I slept in a bit."

"Don't worry, I won't tell the boss."

"That's very kind of you."

"I aim to please. But I hope you have a good excuse," he teased. She almost blushed at the quick memory of his very capable hands all over her naked body all night long. "How are you feeling this morning?"

"Tired, sore, very sore. You?" she asked.

"Not sore, not tired."

"Show off," she said playfully.

"Did you enjoy yourself last night?" he asked.

"Yes I did, very much, and you?"

He smirked, raising his brow to make his point, "You know I did," he said softly.

"May I?" she asked before entering his office.

"By all means, come in, have a seat."

"Nice office, nice power desk. He who sits at the power desk has the power, right?"

"Not necessarily."

Their eyes connected. She took a deep breath and decided to just dive right into the conversation. "About last night, I think we need to clear the air."

"Fine, what part did you want to clear up?"

"I'm not promiscuous by nature. I don't just sleep with perfect strangers. What happened between us last night was a new experience for me. I keep my personal life and my professional life very separate."

"I see."

"Just so that we understand each other," she offered.

"We do," he said smiling.

"I have a question…" she began.

"Is this part of an interview?" he asked.

"No, it's a question about last night." He nodded and motioned for her to continue. "How and when did I get into your bedroom? Oh, and why?"

"You don't remember?" he asked, surprised by the query.

"Believe me, I remember absolutely everything that happened. I just don't remember walking to your room, how did…"

"You didn't walk, I carried you. The when would be shortly after you grabbed the condoms from the drawer in the guest room. I don't have or keep condoms in my bedroom here."

"Okay, so why your bedroom?"

"Contrary to what you might have read about me, or think you know about me, I'm not the player or womanizer everyone seems to think I am. I'm not a saint either, but it is a title I use when needed. This is my grandfather's home, you are his guest. I didn't want housekeeping walking in on us, me naked in your bed. They know not to go into my bedroom unless specifically requested."

"So you were protecting my honor?" she questioned.

"Is that so hard to believe?" he asked earnestly.

She paused to consider. "No, I guess not. Thank you."

"You're welcome," he said.

They sat smiling at each other then Jo suddenly began chuckling. "I can't believe I did that last night."

"Which part?" he asked.

"Any of it, all of it," she said.

"It was something we both needed and wanted," he said as he walked around the desk and sat on the edge in front of her. He picked up an envelope and handed it to her. She nodded. "And when dawn came it was over," he added.

"Right, no strings, one night until dawn." She opened the envelope and began looking through the pages. As she suspected, it was from Jacob.

"Actually, I was just thinking about our little bargain last night," Andre began. "It's a shame we didn't leave room for possible amendments."

She looked up from the pages. The look on his face was pure seduction. "Amendments such as what?" she asked with interest.

"I don't know," he said casually, as if the thought just occurred to him, "perhaps a more open-ended arrangement."

"You mean another night together?" she asked boldly.

"You're right, perhaps that would be asking for trouble. We did say no emotional ties."

"Well," she considered as she stood and leaned back against the desk beside him. "I'm not exactly the kind of woman who needs or even wants attachments. I'm a loner, remember. I don't like to be tied down."

He smiled. "Actually we didn't get around to the tied down part last night, but, uh, if you're game…" he joked.

She leaned her shoulder into him and bumped his arm. "Cute. You know what I mean," Jo said as she stood and walked around to the side of his desk. She picked up a magazine with Daniel Buchanan on the cover. She opened it and flipped through.

"Yes, I do, and I'm not exactly known for my steadfast attachments either." He mimicked her action, standing at the opposite side of the desk watching her.

"Are you suggesting we modify our original arrangement?" she asked nonchalantly without looking up.

He smiled. "But of course we should think about it, and if either of us decides it's not a viable option, then one night will have to be enough," Andre suggested.

She stopped flipping and looked at him, nodding slowly. "You mentioned open-ended, for how long exactly?"

He shrugged with ease. "Any suggestions?" he asked.

"How about only until Jacob returns," Jo said, replacing the magazine then walking to sit behind the large desk. He nodded his agreement.

"Ready?"

"What, you mean right now?" she asked, not sure she was up to more sex with him after last night.

"Ready for another day in Juneau?"

"Actually yes and no, I need to hit the city archives and main library. It's all boring research, verification and corroboration stuff, a lot of books and documents to examine. You don't have to come."

"Are you sure?" he asked.

"Yes, it'll take most of the day, so maybe we can continue the tour tomorrow."

He nodded. "Sounds good."

"One more thing," she said. "I need to borrow a car."

"Sure, I'll get the keys."

She nodded, sitting comfortably behind the power desk wondering what had just happened. Did they just negotiate more nights together at least until Jacob's return? But nothing was final. They had the opportunity to think about it. But really, what was there to think about? There's no way she could repeat what happened last night. It would be madness, not to mention career suicide.

A moment of weakness was all she could fathom as an excuse. Lust, desire, loneliness, temptation, curiosity, the feel of a man holding and caressing her, there was no rational justification for jeopardizing a job. She knew all Andre had to do was expose their night and it would be all over for her professionally. She knew he wanted to stop the bio and get rid of her and she'd given him the ammunition to do it. But for some reason she trusted him. She didn't know why, she just did.

An hour later she sat in Juneau's archive library with her laptop. Oddly enough she focused and got a lot done, working all afternoon and into the early evening. She drove back to the cabin. Andre wasn't there. She went to her bedroom and worked late into the night, trying desperately to keep her mind on her job and avoiding doing anything stupid like going across the hall and jumping into bed with him.

Chapter 13

The second tour of Juneau was just as amazing as the first. As Andre promised, the tour lasted all morning and into late afternoon. They moved quickly, setting a swift pace which, thankfully for Jo because of a sleepless night, kept personal conversation to a minimum.

By the time they were ready to leave Juneau, Jo was completely exhausted. They did everything he said they'd do, plus they'd stopped at Gold Creek and a brewery. The afternoon ended with shopping. Andre insisted on purchasing a replacement outfit for her since her outfit had been ruined in a sudden downpour that caught them by surprise.

"Do you mind if we make one last stop before heading back to the cabin?"

"No, not at all," she said, admiring the scenic view along the coastal Glacier Highway as they drove away from suburban Mendenhall Valley toward downtown

Juneau. They drove across the Juneau-Douglas Bridge and turned right as usual, but drove past Jacob's turnoff and headed farther down along the coast. Jo dozed off as they arrived at a dirt road at the base of a mountain.

Andre made a few turns then continued down a newly paved road until they came to a two-story chalet much smaller than Jacob's. He parked along the side of the building. When Jo woke up they were parked alongside a house she didn't recognize. "Where are we?" she asked. They got out and walked up the path to the front door. "Who lives here?"

Andre opened door then stepped aside allowing her to enter. "I do," he said, closing the door behind them. "Make yourself at home. I need to take care of some business. Look around, I'll be right back," Andre said.

Jo looked around and was impressed by everything she saw. Although much smaller then Jacob's cabin, Andre's home was every bit as impressive. She stepped down into the sunken living room, walked over and stood at the mantel above the fireplace then turned and looked around. The place seemed to be designed precisely with Andre in mind. With clean lines, everything was masculinely tasteful, yet eclectically styled. She could definitely see his influence here.

Jo continued into the dining room and paused at the wall of windows with a glass door. With curtains drawn back, the view was spectacular. Juneau was laid out before her. She walked over and opened the sliding glass door and stepped outside onto the deck. She walked to the rail and looked back up at the side of the mountain. The view as the sun set was sensational. It was as if everything was suspended in time. The sun enhanced the scenery, with its lush greens, piercing blues and fiery reds. The world around her was ablaze with vibrancy. She couldn't help but be awed by the spectacle.

With her hands braced on the rail, she stood completely consumed by the stilled panoramic beauty of the moment. Across the Gastineau Channel she could see the lights of Juneau as evening descended. Eclipsed by the mountainous terrain behind it, the city seemed to glow even as it sparkled in the water between the two land masses. Jo's thoughts began to wander. How could anything be so perfectly mesmerizing? The placid calm she felt lulled her to a peaceful place she hadn't been in a long time.

Lately her days were rushed and tedious as she balanced moments of sanity and craziness. She wrote steadily and her clients were mostly egotistical snobs wanting the world to praise them for their absurdity. Thankfully Jacob wasn't like that.

She smiled, daydreaming wistfully about what it would be like to live here and experience this every day, to wait for Andre to come home to her and then to make love to him all night long. She closed her eyes remembering the feel of his body, the scent of his cologne, the taste of his mouth. Everything about him made her want him. But she knew the danger of mixing business with pleasure. She'd weakened once, and nearly weakened last night, but she had no intention of doing it again. So, for as long as this moment lasted, she'd enjoy it just as it was.

Andre watched her knowing the effect the view would have. The awesome beauty had a way of weakening senses and exaggerating the feeling of euphoria. "Tell me about sign language," he asked.

Jo turned, slightly startled by the deep voice breaking her peaceful trance. "What do you want to know?" she asked and signed the question to him.

He smiled and walked over to the rail to stand beside her. "When did you learn how to do it?"

She moved one hand into the other then finger spelled the letters H and S. She closed and drew her fingers across the front of her body then continued by clapping her hands softly while moving the upper hand in circular motion then raising it up higher. "In high school and college," she said, signing at the same time. "I had a close friend who was hearing impaired and he taught me some basic signs. I became interested and took classes."

"Are you fluent?"

"I can easily hold a conversation, so I'd say I was proficient. I'm not sure I'm ready to translate at the United Nations."

He watched her hands as they quickly communicated her words as she spoke. "That's very impressive."

"Thank you," she signed without speaking by touching her hand to her lips then lowering it and nodding.

"Thank you," he translated easily. She nodded. "How do you sign you're welcome?" She showed him. He repeated her action exactly.

"Very good," she said. "You catch on quickly."

"You're a good teacher," he said turning to look out at the view. "So tell me, how do you like my world?"

"I love it, the view is breathtaking."

He nodded. "This is my favorite time of day."

"I can see why. It's so beautiful."

"You are," he said, leaning back against the rail and gazing at her. She looked away quickly. "Did I offend you?"

"No, I just don't want…"

"Actually," he cut her off quickly, "there's another view that's even more awesome. Would you like to see it?" She looked at him skeptically. He saw her hesitation. "I'm not talking about the view from my bedroom if that's what you think. Come on." He turned and walked down the deck steps, she followed. They came to a garage. He opened it and went inside.

"A dune buggy," she said, "are you kidding?"

"It's the only way to get there. We need to hurry or we'll miss it." He climbed in and turned to her waiting with a smile on his face.

"What's with you and these half vehicles? Can't you guys afford a whole car or truck or something?"

He laughed. "Come on, get in. Trust me. You don't want to miss this."

Jo climbed in and buckled up as Andre backed up and sped away. She held on tight as the jumping jarring ride knocked her around like a rag doll. "Are you okay?" Andre yelled over the loud motor.

"Hardly," she yelled her response while still laughing.

"Hold on, we're almost there." He floored the accelerator, splashing water up all around them. A few minutes later they came to the edge of a sandy beach. He continued driving until he got to a place just where the water met the land. He sped through, causing another huge splash of cold water to spray around them. Soaked, she screamed and laughed all at the same time. Seconds later he spun the vehicle around and stopped. Breathless she looked at him wondering what to expect. Then she saw it. Amazement gripped her.

She was spellbound at the sight of tiny lights sparkling on the water all around her. They were on land, but it seemed like they were floating in the center of the water. "What is this?" she asked. "What's that noise?"

"Fish. The city lights sparkle and it fools them into thinking it's food. This whole area is a wildlife refuge. Migrant birds and other animals travel through in search of food and breeding grounds." He sat up on the back of the seat. She started to get out. "No," he said, grabbing her arm and holding her back. "We can't stay long. This island will be under water in about ten minutes."

"What do you mean it'll be under water?" she said with some panic in her voice.

"Don't worry, we're fine," Andre laughed. "This small patch of land shows up just before dusk and disappears a few minutes later."

She sat up on the back of her seat as he did and looked all around her. They were completely surrounded by water and reflecting lights. "This is astonishing. How is it possible?"

"I could tell you the scientific story of melting glaciers carved a millennia ago, but somehow it's not as interesting as the locals' stories about ancestors, spirits and rituals."

"This is," she began then just stopped. "I don't know what this is. I've never seen anything like it," she said wrapping her arms around her body for warmth. The air was chilled and the cold water had soaked her.

"My grandfather tells stories about how his father mined gold around here back before the turn of the twentieth century. I'm sure he'll tell you more about that later. Right now we need to leave." He sat down, she did too. He started the engine and they quickly sped away.

By the time they got back to the house, Jo was completely frozen. "That was unbelievable," she said as she shivered and her teeth chattered nonstop.

"Come on," he said, guiding her through the house then upstairs to the master bedroom. "You gotta get warm. I'll run a hot bath." She followed him into his bathroom and he immediately began running water into a huge tub. "Take your clothes off," he said offering her a towel. "I'll be right back." He left the room.

She nodded, shaking involuntarily as she looked over

at the filling tub. It was huge and she couldn't wait to get in. She peeled her clothes off and stood with a towel wrapped around her body.

Andre knocked and returned moments later with a basket of bath supplies. He placed them on the counter then sat on the side of the sunken tub testing the temperature of the water, careful to keep his back to her. She walked over and stood by his side as he waved his hand through the hot water. "Is this okay?" he asked. She dipped her hand in and nodded. "Good, get in," he said as he turned on the massaging jets. The water instantly agitated. He got up and walked to the bathroom door, keeping his back to her.

She smiled at his politeness, removed the towel and got into the tub. The hot water felt wonderful. "You know the whole modesty thing is a moot point after the other night, don't you think? We have seen each other naked."

"That was a mutual arrangement. Taking advantage of a half frozen woman isn't exactly my style." He turned around, certain by now that she was in the tub beneath the steaming water and foaming jets. She was. "Take your time. The knobs on the side work the jets. I'm not sure what's in the basket. I think it might be lotion and other toiletries you might need. I'll leave it here on the counter. I'm gonna change and get us something to eat before we head back to my grandfather's cabin."

Jo nodded and sunk down deeper into the soothing hot water. The heat and massaging jets on her cold stiff body felt like heaven. She closed her eyes and dipped her head back, wetting her hair. She stayed like that a while, letting the water soothe and relax her tired body. When she sat up she was feeling like herself again, rejuvenated. She adjusted the jets and stayed in the tub for over a half an hour. As she lay there naked in the cooling water, she began to think about Andre.

The tub was huge. She wondered what it would be like to have him in there with her, to feel the jets massaging their bodies as they made love. She took the large sea sponge and rubbed it over her breasts stimulating her areola and nipples much like he he'd done two nights before. She closed her eyes and thought about him being in there with her. How his hands would touch her and how his mouth would taste her everywhere.

She turned the jets back up and reveled in her vivid imagination. But the pulsating jets did little to ease her wayward thoughts. She wanted Andre and nothing else would do. The sex with him was incredible, but it wasn't just that. She really enjoyed being with him the last few days. His humor, his intelligence and the fact that they could talk about anything was so different. She opened her eyes quickly realizing that she was beginning to feel too deeply for him.

She was a realist. There was no way she could have a lasting relationship with Andre. That just didn't happen to people like her. They were from two different worlds, his situated halfway up a mountain that he actually owned. When he offered his body to her, she wanted him out of wanton lust. But they'd made a connection and that connection had been growing ever since. Everything he did, everything he said, merely added to her growing feelings.

All her life she made it a point to never get attached to anyone and to never feel what she was feeling now. If she didn't feel, then she didn't get hurt when that person left or turned on her. But now she was worried that it was already too late to pull back. She had opened up to Andre to get him to trust her and she got caught in her own trap.

Realizing that the hot water had cooled and her body had heated, it was time to get out. She released the water, dried herself off with the thick gray towel and went into his bedroom. Half hoping to see Andre in bed waiting for her, she was surprised at how disappointed she was when he wasn't there. Her reaction showed just how much she'd opened to him.

Her thoughts had become single-focused on Andre, the way he touched her and made her body burn. Banishing thoughts obviously wasn't working. She decided to go full speed ahead. She knew he wanted her physically and she wanted him and if that's all she could have of him, then she decided that she'd take it. Since Jacob would probably be back in the next few days, tonight was the perfect time to be with him.

She went back into the bathroom and towel dried her hair. Needing lotion and a comb, she peeked through the cellophane wrap around the basket on the counter. The tag stated that it was a his and hers bath basket. She untied the ribbon and pulled out lotion, a comb and brush. Looking through, she noted a few other things including candles, incense, bubble bath, massage gel and condoms. When she'd finished applying lotion she went back in the bedroom and saw a T-shirt and sweatpants laid out for her on the bed. The clothes were extra large on her and the sweatpants kept slipping down her hips. She looked at herself in the mirror. She wasn't exactly a seductress in this outfit, but she didn't think that mattered. He wanted her, she wanted him. The decision was made. She went downstairs looking for him.

"Why did she have to be so trusting," Andre muttered aloud to himself as he stood beneath a fierce punishing blast of water. He looked up into the stream letting cool water pour down over his face and down his body. The shower started off hot, but he turned up the cold water soon after he began thinking about the woman down the hall lying naked in his tub. As wet and cold as his body had been from being outside, there was no way he could stand a hot shower without exploding.

"Why did you have to be so sexy?" He leaned back against the black tile wall and closed his eyes. His imagination was running wild with the things he could do to her at that moment. He'd bring her into the shower stall. He'd pick her up and have her legs wrap around his waist. With her back against the wall, he would thunder into her as his mouth held firm to her tender orbs of delight. Breathing hard and feeling his body react, he had no choice but to turn the hot water completely off. The shocking result nearly numbed him, but it did the trick.

He got out of the shower much as he got in, nearly frozen. He dried off and dressed quickly. He went down to the kitchen, gathered a cold platter of meats, fruit, cheeses and crackers and made a pot of hot chocolate. He took the platter, chocolate and cups into the living room, turned on the gas fireplace and hoped he was doing the right thing. He sat on the sofa and began re-reading her file sent to him on his BlackBerry earlier. He needed more and it seemed Rhames wasn't working quickly enough.

He was having second thoughts as guilt began to nag at him. What if he was wrong about her? What if she was telling the truth and she was just going to write his grandfather's biography and leave it at that? What if her secrets had nothing to do with the Buchanan family past? Anything was possible. Still, his main concern was protecting his family, even as far back at Louis.

No one knew the truth, it was too far back and records had been lost, burned or just plain destroyed. But rumors and accusations had little to do with the truth. There was no proof either way and that's what concerned him. How do you spin and control ghosts of the past?

"Hi, I'm back," she said.

He turned, switched off his PDA and looked up as she stepped down into the living room. "Hey, how are you feeling?"

"Much better, thanks," she said, sitting down on the sofa beside him. The room was toasty warm from the fireplace and the lighting was dim and romantic. There was one light on in the corner, but it was far enough away and low enough not to brighten the whole room.

He placed his phone on the coffee table beside the food platter. "I guess I shouldn't have taken you out there this evening. I forgot you weren't used to the cold weather."

"No, I loved it. I had a great time."

"Hot chocolate?" he offered, pouring some into a second cup.

"Yes, thanks," she said, taking the cup and sipping the hot drink. The chocolate warmth filled her mouth and eased down her throat. She licked her lips slowly wondering how or if she should go through with what she planned.

"Are you hungry?" he asked as he turned to her.

"Not exactly, are you?"

"No, not really."

"Thanks for the dry clothes. I like the T-shirt, but the sweatpants are a little big. They keep falling down." He smiled, obviously imagining the imagery. She smiled seeing her opening. "Or was that the whole idea?" she asked wilily.

"Not at all. Believe me, I'm not that restrained with my intentions. You should know by now that I find subtlety wastes too much time," Andre said, holding her gaze in a penetrating stare.

She had no intention of looking away. "I totally agree, so let's cut to the chase, shall we?" she said boldly. She placed her cup on the table, stood up and looked down at him. He smiled and that was all she needed. She sat down on his lap, straddling his thighs. His hands came up instinctively to hold her waist. She looked into his eyes, and leaned in intending to kiss him tenderly. But instead, when their lips touched, there was an explosion of passion.

Jo parted her lips and Andre's tongue instantly slipped into her mouth and hers into his. She moaned, feeling her body react to his perfect intrusion. Both forceful and hard, the kiss took complete control of them. Wanting even more she inched closer as his strong arms wrapped tight, holding her in place. She trembled inside as the kiss deepened. Her body shook with desire as his hands squeezed her rear, kneading, massaging, pulsating and pressing her closer and closer to his erection. She rocked her hips to his rhythm. The excitement of the instant seduction had her already teetering on the edge.

She broke the kiss and leaned back breathless staring at him. "Maybe this is going too far, maybe we need to…" she began, and was cut off when he pulled her back to his mouth. This kiss was even more dynamic. She was dizzy with pleasure, her mind swam in delight, drowning, falling helplessly into the swell of passion. She'd never felt so completely in and out of control at the same time.

She grabbed the hem of his T-shirt and pulled it up over his head as he relaxed his hold on her. Ending the kiss, she leaned back again. The sight of his bare chest seemed to always excite her. She spread her hands wide over him, feeling him. Also breathless, he closed his eyes and licked his lips. She tweaked his nipples. From past experience she knew his were just as sensitive as hers. He groaned, and the reaction prompted her further. She nibbled his earlobe and trailed tiny licking kisses down his neck and across his chest. She licked his nipple and felt his body lurch. "You like that?" she muttered playfully. He groaned again. "You want more?" she asked.

In an instant he grabbed the bottom of her shirt and pulled it up and tossed it. She watched his reaction with a smile. It was obvious that the sight of her full breasts and pebbled nipples stiffened his already hard erection. She felt his penis harden even more if that was even possible. He was ready, but still he held back. He cupped her breasts, her head rolled back and her body arched, thrusting her chest out to him. The action made her pants slip down to her hips now held up solely because her legs were spread open straddling him.

She held on to his shoulders as his hands gathered her breasts together and his mouth connected. She gasped seeing his luscious appetite as he devoured her so completely. The instant sensation of seeing and feeling took her breath away. Ravenous at first, then he was slow and methodical, torturing her with his mouth, driving her to near madness. "Andre, upstairs?" she muttered.

He stopped and looked down the length of her seeing tiny curled hair teasing him from just below the waistband. With one hand firmly pressed to her back he traced his fingers down the front of her ending just as the hairs began. "Let's go upstairs," she muttered again looking into his willful eyes.

He shook his head. "We'd never make it." He grabbed her rear and pressed her closer to his body. "Nice outfit," he muttered.

She smiled seductively feeling the place between her legs getting wetter still. "I think we have too many clothes on."

"I can fix that." He leaned in and kissed her as he reached to the sides and began unsnapping her sweats. She was so focused on his mouth and his tongue that she didn't even realize what he was doing with his hands until she was completely naked. The kiss ended. She looked down at her body realizing that she hadn't moved, but was completely naked on top of him.

"Nice trick, got any others?"

"How about this one?" He lifted her up and eased her to lie down on the sofa. She spread her legs anticipating him joining her. He didn't. "Close your eyes," he whispered near her ear.

"Why?" she asked, closing her eyes as he requested.

"I want to kiss you," he whispered, "here," pressing his mouth to her forehead, and then trailing down to her cheek and ear. "And maybe here," he continued kissing her neck and shoulder.

"Andre…"

"Sh," he hushed her.

"Andre…"

"And here too," he kissed her chest then each breast. She gasped when he licked one nipple then the other. Her body shuddered and trembled.

"Andre, what are you going to do?" she asked, with her eyes still obediently closed.

"What do you think I'm going to do?" he asked, licking her nipple causing her to moan with pleasure. "Do you like that?" he asked. "Or do you like this," he asked as the flat of his tongue barely touching her then he licked her other nipple. She quivered and tried to withdraw. "Do you want me to stop?" he asked.

She shook her head. "No, don't stop," she rasped. He raised her hand to his lips and kissed each finger then placed it above her head. He repeated the action with her other hand. She lay stretched out, her arms above her head and her eyes closed. But instead of feeling vulnerable and powerless, she felt in complete control. Ordinarily, she never would have agreed to something like this, but his voice calmed her and made her want more.

"Do you trust me to give you pleasure?" he whispered close to her ear. She nodded without speaking. "Will you do as I ask?" She nodded again. "Then relax and let me please you."

She nodded and instantly felt him touch her lips. His finger traced to her forehead, down her cheek and down her neck following the trail of kisses earlier. When he touched her breasts she shivered as every nerve seemed to scream. She felt the sensation tenfold when his finger traced down her stomach to rest between her legs.

"You're wet," he whispered deep and throaty, "good, 'cause I think I'm hungry now." He opened her legs and leaned in. "Enough."

Her eyes popped open. She looked down and saw him just before his mouth touched her. She had no idea what he meant by the word *enough*, and at this point she wasn't sure she cared. Her thoughts faded and her mind went to mush. His mouth was there. She gasped and attempted to close her legs, but he was there already too firmly entrenched in the purposeful pleasure of her body. "Andre," she whispered, her throat dry from panting. He didn't answer. He was too busy giving her pleasure. "Andre," she called out again as his tongue penetrated. She moaned and twitched each time he stroked her.

He licked and sucked the tiny nib and the spot just above it. She felt her body teeter on the edge of what was probably every cell in her brain exploding. Her legs shook. Her body tensed. How could she take any more of this? But she could and at one point she even opened her legs wider. He instantly took advantage of the invitation. His actions became more intense. He lifted her rear off the sofa and delved deep into her.

She bit at her lower lip and held her breath trying not to scream. She moaned and writhed, coming closer and closer to the edge. She gasped then exploded into a million blinding pieces. He continued. Her body bucked with a second intense spasm, then another and another. "Andre," she called his name. Still he continued. She exploded again, screaming out. This time the orgasm was even more powerful as her body shook uncontrollably. "Andre, Andre, enough," she rasped breathlessly. He stopped. Jo felt herself release. With her eyes still closed she wondered if her body was still in one piece. It took her several minutes to compose herself.

"That was incredible," she moaned, "you're incredible."

"Actually incredible is what happens next." Andre stood and held his hand out to her. Curious, she took his hand and stood. She grabbed the T-shirt, slipped it on and followed him upstairs to his bathroom. He removed his sweats, opened the tinted shower door and stepped inside. A dim light began to glow. Instead of stopping, he kept going, turning a corner and disappearing from sight.

"This is a shower, right?" she asked.

"Come on," he called out to her.

Jo grabbed some condoms from the basket on the counter and followed him inside the shower stall. She peeked around the corner curiously. There was a sudden chill, like an outside door opening. She found him standing in the connecting outside shower.

"Incredible…" Jo gasped, looking around then up at the open sky. The view was amazing, but being out there was totally insane. The outside shower stall itself was the size of an extra large closet. To one side was a curved alcove and a padded seat. With a surrounding surface of black and gray marble tile and chrome, it was simply gorgeous. She watched as he turned on the water. "You realize that you're outside, right?" she joked.

There was a waterfall-like effect against the back tiled wall. She marveled at the ingenuity. He turned a few more knobs and several showerheads released jets of water all around them as well as a warm misting steam from the rim above. The surrounding lights dimmed and the iridescent tiles seemed to shimmer and glow beneath the stars. "I guess just a simple shower stall with one showerhead was totally out of the question."

He nodded. "Totally," he said, curling his finger and motioning for her to come to him. "Come on out."

His intent was obvious. She shook her head laughing. "No way."

"Trust me."

"Are you kidding, I'll freeze out there. It's like minus two degrees. You're used to this weather—I'm not."

"Trust me," he repeated with added sincerity, "I promise if you get the least bit chilly we'll go back inside."

He was the perfect temptation. She smiled, biting her lower lip, considering his offer. Then shaking her head, she stepped outside and walked to him drinking in the magnificence of his body. His erection was still hard and jutting straight out to her. She walked over and stood right up against his body. He helped her remove her T-shirt. Her pebbled nipples brushed against him with each breath she took. He was right. She didn't feel the chill. Warm water poured down his chest and sprayed over her shoulder and down her back. The hot steam mist surrounded them like a floating cloud. She looked around then up through the hot steam.

The sky sparkled like jewels thrown across the black velvet. There was no chill, no cold, there was only the heat of her body and his surrounded by the warmth of hot steam and warm flowing water.

Andre leaned down and kissed her slowly, deliberately taking his time as his hands caressed her back lovingly. She felt her body go weak as she wrapped her arms around his neck and held tight. When the kiss ended she stepped back. Looking over his lean muscled body, she smiled. His erection was full and hard. She grasped him, ringing her hand around him firmly. His quick intake was expected. She pulled through the length of his shaft ending with a slight twist to the tip. He pulled her to his body instantly and kissed her hard then looked intently into her eyes. "We're playing with fire here, you know that don't you?" he said huskily.

She smiled seductively. "Definitely." She opened the condom packet and put it on him. They kissed again as he lifted her up and she wrapped her legs around his waist and held tight. He took a few steps forward, pressing her back against the warm waterfall wall. In one smooth action, he lifted her higher then slowly entered her. She gasped and held tight, releasing a tiny moan.

The intense sensual feeling of his throbbing erection inside of her took her breath away. He'd filled her completely then stopped. They looked into each other's eyes knowing that they'd gone way past the point of unemotional. This wasn't just sex as they promised. She wasn't sure if it ever was.

Slow and deliberate he began to move in and out of her, rocking his hips up and down pressing her firmly against the shower's waterfall. A steady stream of warm water poured over her shoulders as their eyes stayed connected. The pure rapture of the moment was beyond words. They were each caught in a fantasy of their making as the swell of climax began to build.

The hot steam swirled and billowed around them, caressing their bodies as the ecstasy continued to build. Each pleasurable thrust was gentle and firm. The intense sensuousness of their lovemaking was mind-blowing as the slow steady rapture consumed them. Their breathing quickened to swift gasps. Eye to eye they reached that point. The edge was here, the crest had peaked. Then they both burst. She held tight, feeling his body tremble and shake. It was too much and not nearly enough.

Trembling and shaking from the mind-shattering climax, they stood wrapped together tightly. In an instant this rapturous pleasure had defined what lovemaking would always be for them, adventurous, trusting, undaunted and passionate. He kissed her, letting his tongue linger lovingly on her lips. She embraced the sensuousness of his intimate touch.

Afterward they stood holding each other as the pulsating water streamed down their bodies. Both breathless and motionless, they were wrapped together. With her still in his arms, he walked over and sat on the padded seat. Face-to-face, he sat with her still straddling his lap. It seemed to be their favorite position. His kiss trailing down her neck to her chest. She arched back, resting her hands on his knees. He took her nipple into his mouth and suckled as she opened another condom packet and put it on him.

"Your breasts are pure succulence."

"I think you like that," she said impaling herself on him.

"I do. They're the perfect appetizer." He nibbled her until she started squirming.

Jo licked her lips. She could feel him getting hard again. This time he was already inside of her, so the sensation of his erection growing and throbbing inside of her was intense. It was the start of another thirty minutes of sultry, steaming lovemaking.

Later Jo lay across Andre's bed on her stomach with her chin resting on her folded arms. She watched the crackling fire in the fireplace as Andre sat up on his elbow, stroking and caressing her back and buttocks lovingly. After the shower they snacked on the cold platter of food and drank a bottle of wine before retiring to the bed. Jo sighed. "Did I mention that you're incredible?" she asked, closing her eyes sleepily.

He kissed the small of her back and snuggled close. "Yes, I believe you did," he said, looking down on his almost sleeping beauty. Just seeing her lying there on his bed caused his body to react. He wanted her all over again. But he knew she was tired. They'd had a full day, then making love had worn her out.

He, however, was wide awake. He lay there stroking her back and caressing her buttocks and thinking about the moment she finds out this was all just a distraction to keep her away from his grandfather and his family's past. He began to feel guilty again.

It had started perfectly, but then he opened his heart to seal her trust and found that she'd gotten to him. He'd fallen in love with her and he knew there was no way he could continue doing what he was doing without tearing them both apart.

He knew what it felt like to be used and he couldn't betray her like this. His ex-wife had used him solely to gain access to Titan for her father. She pretended to love him, but it was all just a lie. It tore him apart and he didn't want to do that to Jo.

Chapter 14

Jo quietly slid out of bed and slipped on the T-shirt she wore earlier. Without the sagging sweats this time, she walked over to stand at the balcony doors. She couldn't sleep, her feelings were too jumbled. Adrenaline pumped through her body at warp speed. Her mind was a whirlwind of confusing thoughts, some elation, some cautionary and some just plain troubled. The latter being the most prominent. Everything she thought she knew about herself had changed. She never felt like this before. The sudden sensation of emotion was overwhelming. She was in love with Andre and her world had been turned upside down in just days.

She turned and looked back at Andre sleeping peacefully. With the fireplace still burning and candles flickering on the bedside table, the room had a shadowy glow. The setting was romantic and seductive. Being here with him felt so right. But this wasn't supposed to be, they weren't supposed to be. She looked away quickly.

She was tempted to slide the door open and step outside into the night air, but she knew the sudden blast of cold air would wake him up. Instead she looked at her reflection. It was perfectly clear, but still she didn't recognize the image. The no-nonsense, isolated loner she always claimed to be was nowhere in sight. Before coming to Alaska she prided herself on never letting anyone get close to her and never getting close to others. The uncomplicated focus had worked all her life. If no one cared for her, then she didn't need to care for them back. Somewhere along the line things got complicated and she lost that focus.

She cared, she loved, and now she found herself feeling very different. She'd lost herself in emotion and she had no idea how to handle it. Her heart was beginning to rule her head. Her comfort zone had been breached and she let it. All her life she took risks, but never with the heart. Now she was taking the biggest risk she could possibly fathom. She had opened herself up and given her heart to a man she barely knew, and now she was in love.

Andre wasn't the same man she met in the foyer and in the library. Something had changed, he changed. She could handle arrogant and cocky. She was used to men like that, but now he was open and loving. How could she steel her heart against that, against feelings, against love?

She shifted her focus. She needed this job and falling for her client's grandson was not supposed to happen. But she knew that it already had. She was exhausted and vulnerable. She'd been running away all her life from something she never thought she'd find, love. Then when she stopped running Andre was there.

She thought about the horrendous situation with her last biography assignment almost a year ago. The senator's husband was convincing, and had she not walked in on him and the senator's aide, she would have believed it herself when he denied it. Then instead of taking responsibility, he accused her of coming on to him. So much for integrity. She told the truth, but everyone believed him. After all, he was rich, handsome and the husband of a powerful politician. She was only a writer who'd found out the truth and that truth could destroy careers, hers included.

She looked beyond her image at the muted darkness, knowing that she would never forget last night. They fit so perfectly and after the shower they had talked until she nodded off.

She looked up. The sky sparkled with a billion stars glowing brightly above the Juneau city lights. The sight was just as breathtaking at night as it was in day. This was an amazing place. She wondered how it all began.

She knew the text history of course. There were thousands of books written about Alaskan history. She read dozens herself. But she of all people knew that the real truth was seldom written as such. Man wrote as he wanted to be remembered, not as he was. The actions were glorified, personas were embellished and deeds were larger-than-life. The truth was oftentimes far from that.

It was probably true of Louis Buchanan, one of the original settlers of this land. Everything she read and heard from Jacob pointed to one conclusion. He was a formidable man with an iron will. She wondered what trials he went through as a black man in this harsh wilderness—racial injustice, bigotry, segregation. She speculated that he was indeed a strong man with a will of iron and a powerful resolve. Anyone weaker would have never survived and become so powerful.

She began to wonder what he really looked like. Jacob had several old photos in the boxes he'd given her to look at, but none were identified. There was one photo that came to mind. She remembered it well. Sepia faded monochrome, there were eight men standing in front of an old wooden structure. Five were white, two black and one Indian.

She remembered looking at the two black men, scrutinizing their faces with a purpose. The eyes, mouth and noses were different as was everything else. The build was wrong, the stance was off. They couldn't have been related to the Buchanan men she saw in recent photos. Nothing about those men showed it.

But to her surprise, one man in the photo could have easily been Jacob's twin. The resemblance was startling. He was dusty, muddy and dirty as he peered from beneath a wide brimmed hat. The facial features were almost exact. But the man was most definitely white and by all accounts Louis was black. It couldn't have been Louis. She looked up at the sky and wondered more about the men in the old tattered photo.

She stood in silence surrounded in darkness and staring out into the night. She seemed so lost. Like a child wading too far from shore, tossed into the deep. His first instinct was to go to her, but instead he lay there watching, wondering what she was thinking. She was a mystery, and from the first moment he saw her in the airport he was attracted to her. Bold and passionate at times, shy and withdrawn at others, he had no idea who the real woman was.

He knew that he admired her. She was different than other women he knew. She had passion and fire and an inner inquisitiveness and fascination for life he had forgotten even existed. She seemed interested in everything and saw life as a possibility rather than a futility. It was that excitement and difference that drew him in. He just didn't know how much.

He did know that his father and uncles were right. Her job here needed to end. No one should know about the

Buchanan past. It should be buried with the last of them. But he also knew that time would eventually catch up with them. Family scandals were big business. The more notable the family, the more the media sensationalized the scandal. His family wasn't immune. They'd had scandals in the past. But the real scandal was the truth about his family's beginnings and that truth was buried deep in the attic and basements of the family home. But Andre knew that nothing stays buried forever, not secrets and not even the truth.

What's the worst that could happen?

Jo turned and saw Andre sitting up in bed, the sheet casually draped across his legs. It looked as if he was deep in thought. She smiled and shook her head, damned if he didn't look too sexy sitting there. "Hey," she said seductively, walking back to the bed.

"Hey yourself," Andre said, seeing her approach in the darkness, "can't sleep?"

She shrugged and shook her head. "Sometimes it's like that. When it is I either get up in the middle of the night and work, or I just sit and look out the window."

"What's so interesting looking out at the night?" he asked.

"The sky, I love looking out at the night sky. It's so limitless with endless possibilities. And here in Alaska it's even more so. We're all so small and insignificant compared to the power of all that. It makes you believe anything is possible."

"Anything is possible," he assured her.

"Not for some people," she said.

"You want to tell me about it?"

"Tell you about what?" she asked evasively.

"About whatever's troubling you."

"What makes you think something's troubling me?" she asked. He smiled his answer. "Lucky guess," she said, sitting on the side of the bed. She shook her head and half smiled as she kissed him tenderly. "Tell me something, why are you so different now?"

"You mean different from the spoiled, arrogant self-centered jerk before?" he asked. She grimaced knowing that he was paraphrasing her words. She nodded slowly. "I don't know. I think it has something to do with you being here."

"You mean our, *no ties, no strings, uncommitted, pure mutual physical pleasure just sex,* turned you into a new man? I doubt that."

"Well, maybe it has something to do with the rules of engagement changing. Uncomplicated has suddenly gotten complicated and just sex isn't just sex for either of us, is it?"

She shook her head. "No. But where does that lead us?"

"I don't know yet, but for right now it leads you to tell me what's bothering you. Maybe I can help," he prompted.

She sighed and looked away, "Ghosts."

"Past or present?"

"Both."

"Ah, the worst kind, the ones you know and the ones you see coming but can't do anything about. Is there anything I can do to ease your troubles, silence the ghosts?"

"No, just being here with you helps," she said, "thank you. I guess I need to take back all the things I said about you."

"You mean I'm not still an arrogant self-centered jerk?"

"Well, maybe not the jerk part," she joked. They laughed.

"Come here," he whispered softly. She moved closer. He leaned down and kissed her tenderly. Afterward he looked into her eyes and gently touched the side of her face. "This wasn't the plan."

"What plan? What do you mean?" she asked.

"It doesn't matter. What matters is that everything's changed. You changed it. I never meant to feel this way, but I do. I love you," he said.

She beamed happily. "That's great, because I love you too."

He pulled her gently into his arms and kissed her lovingly. Then they lay back, cocooned in their new love. She closed her eyes and sighed as he held her tight and stroked her back.

"Mmm, this feels so right," she whispered.

Andre wrapped his arms tighter as she snuggled closer. The realization didn't hit him as hard as he expected, but she was right, being here together did feel right. None of this was supposed to be real, at least on his part, but now it was. He loved her, but he had also manipulated her. He feared that everything she was feeling he had manipulated to get rid of her, or at the very least keep her distracted in order to perpetuate the Buchanan lie.

Andre opened his eyes when he heard Jo's steady, even breathing. She was asleep. He was awake. There's no way he could sleep after his confession. A part of him wished it was a lie, but it wasn't. He did love her. The question now was how could he protect his family and love her at the same time? It was impossible. The troubling thoughts continued to run through his mind until he dozed off.

A few hours later Andre woke up again. This time the touch of dawn had just tipped over the horizon. Stiff and tired, his body protested the early hour, but he knew he had to get up. He'd been off schedule for the last few days. It was time to get back to it. He looked down at the woman curled around him in his bed, the cause for his recently disrupted schedule. She was definitely worth it.

He smiled remembering their night of passion. Last night was the most exciting night he could remember. Slow and deliberate, they'd made love. Their bodies meshed, but it was way past the physical act. Waking up beside her, reaching for her in the night and having her there made it clear.

She'd gotten to him and damned if he wasn't letting her. He got up, showered and dressed in sweats to go for a run and clear his clouded thoughts. The cold morning mountain air always invigorated him. It had a way of slicing through hesitation and confusion and refocusing his energy. He needed that today.

Everything about his current objective had been compromised. Not only was he second-guessing his motives, but he was second-guessing his job. Being wrong about someone was never an issue he considered. Neither was falling in love. He'd raised the red flag to his family about Jo, they'd agreed, now he wanted to reverse course four days in. He shook his head. He really needed to refocus.

"Hey, good morning, you leaving me already?" she asked, seeing him sitting across the room tying his running shoes.

"Good morning," he said, smiling up at her, admiring the delectable sight of her lying in his big bed after a night of lovemaking. He could definitely get used to seeing her there on a more permanent basis. "How'd you sleep?"

"Great. You're my hero, you chased the ghosts away."

"That's what heroes do," he joked.

"You know, you're pretty handy to have around."

"I'm glad you think so," he said, as he walked over and stood beside the bed. "Maybe I'll hang around a lot more. What do you think?"

"I think I'd like that. Last night was a dream. I can hardly believe any of it was real."

He eased down beside her. "You weren't dreaming. It was all real, everything, even the part when I told you that I love you."

She smiled warmly. Hearing the words from him again was like the beginning of a new world for her. "I love you too. I think I just wanted to hear you say it again. So, are you going for a run?" she asked. He nodded. "How long are you going to be?"

"Two hours tops, afterward I'm going to grab breakfast for us. There's nothing in the house except coffee. And if I'm gonna have you in my bed all day I think we might need some nourishment," he said, leaning over to kiss her shoulder. "We have things to do."

"In bed all day?" she asked, as he continued kissing her shoulder arm and neck. "And what if I already have plans? I do have a job to do. And what about your job, don't you need to right the wrongs against the Buchanan family?"

"Not today. Today is solely for me. The only job I have is to make love to you over and over and over again." He smiled greedily as he licked his lips and lovingly stroked her thigh and waist.

"Ah, a hero's noble sacrifice. Well, in that case I guess the least I could do is make the coffee, give you a taste of my more domestic side," she said seductively.

"That's not the side I'm interested in at the moment." He pulled the sheet down, revealing her breasts with nipples already hard. He smiled as soon as he saw the unveiling. "Now that's what I call a morning eye opener. I think I'll skip the run and have breakfast right here, right now." He dipped down and captured her nipple in his mouth.

She giggled and moved away. "No, go, run and get breakfast. I'll be here waiting when you get back."

"Don't move. I'll be right back," he whispered close as he looked down the length of her body smiling and shaking his head admiringly. She was too tempting. "An hour and a half," he said.

"Wait, I have my flash drive with me and I need to write some notes. Can I use your computer if I promise not to snoop?"

Andre went still. His ex-wife got into his computer without asking and nearly destroyed his family. He looked into Jo's joyous sparkling eyes. There was no deceit or betrayal, only love. Like never before, this was a test of his trust. Both his mind and heart told him that Jo wouldn't betray him. "Sure. It's in the office downstairs."

"Thanks, it'll only take forty-five minutes, I promise. I'll meet you in the tub afterward."

"In that case, I'll be back in an hour," he promised. He gave her a quick kiss, then got up and hurried out.

Jo chuckled as she watched him leave. His humorous hastened retreat only added to her love for him. He made her feel so good. She had opened her heart and he was there to protect and cherish it. She rolled over and looked up at the skylight. It was still mostly dark outside since the sun had barely tipped the horizon, but she already knew it was going to be a fantastic day. A giggle bubbled inside then came out as tearful joy. She couldn't help herself. For the first time in her life she felt happy, really happy.

She closed her eyes, feeling the anger and pain she had held onto for so long wash away. She was ready to stop running and it was a relief. For so long she carried around the emotional scars of her past. Insecurities and apprehension ruled her life and made her vulnerable. In defense, she had closed herself down emotionally. But now this was a brand-new day. No more drama, no more secrets and no more pain. She found a man who would not use and betray her.

She got up feeling incredible. She knew nothing could possibly bring her down. She went to the bathroom and immediately saw the large sunken tub in the center of the room. The idea of being in there with Andre got her excited all over again.

She grabbed a quick shower and put on her clothes. Afterward she went downstairs to the kitchen to make coffee for Andre's return. She found the home office and sat down at the computer. She inserted her flash drive and started typing. The phone rang. She ignored the message being left until she heard her name mentioned. She stopped cold. Her heart sank as her head pounded, nearly blinding her. Gasping, panting, she couldn't breathe. Instantly an e-mail message screen popped up. She read the message, but didn't open the attachments. She didn't have to. She already knew what they were. They were her life. She went back upstairs to get dressed. It was time to leave.

Chapter 15

A quick rush of cold air hit Andre as soon as he stepped outside. He took a deep breath and released it slowly as he looked around. Seeing Juneau the past few days with Jo had given him a new insight into his home. He'd taken it for granted, not seeing the beauty all around him. He looked up at the mountains, behind them a brand-new day. The idea of spending it with Jo made him smile. Then the idea of spending it in a sunken tub with her made him hard.

He stretched, walked down the steps and started his run. Taking his usual route, he ran down the main road, across the dirt path down through the thicket of trees which would lead him along the water's edge. The clarity of his thoughts and feelings intensified as he ran. He'd been waiting for Jo all his life. She was exactly what he needed.

The run was even shorter than he expected. Twenty-five minutes in to it his cell phone rang. He slowed and answered breathlessly. It was Ben Rhames. "Good, I caught you running."

"Yeah, you have something for me?" Andre asked, slowing even more, but keeping a steady, even pace.

"Yeah, I have your father on the other line, I'll patch him through."

"Good morning, son, looks like you were right. We have problems," Daniel said as soon as the connection was set.

"What's going on?" Andre asked.

"I've already discussed this with your father. It looks like Ms. Butler has more to hide than we thought. She got into some legal problems," Ben said.

"What kind of legal problems?" Andre asked.

"A lot of it's unsubstantiated, but I'm still working on it."

"Tell him what you have so far," Daniel said.

Ben proceeded to tell Andre about his preliminary findings. He started off with personal information then got into more details. The more he relayed, the slower Andre ran. After a while he stopped and just listened. The information was far more damaging than he expected. Apparently Jo's past was more checkered than she had let on.

"Are you absolutely sure about this last part?" Andre asked.

"Positive. A high-powered D.C. attorney filed suit against her. The proceedings were closed for privacy of course and there's a gag order, but my information is on target."

"What was the suit about?" he asked.

"I'm hearing everything from attempted blackmail to an accomplice to the desolation of marriage to theft, libel and perpetration of fraud. There's a lot of hearsay and rumors, but no one knows for sure because of the gag order. I do know that before going to the grand jury, a major portion of the suit was dropped. Afterward the judge ordered all her files relinquished and reviewed. Ms. Butler refused. She appealed and lost, subsequently she turned the files over to the court. It seemed power, money and political influence won the day."

Andre remembered Jo talking about her loathing for people with power and money, and the deliberate way they influenced others. "So there's nothing substantial."

"I call fraud, libel and blackmail pretty substantial charges. Sounds to me like she had an affair with her client then tried to blackmail him. Do you know who the attorneys represented?" Daniel asked.

"A U.S. senator, that's all I know for sure."

"A politician," Andre muttered to himself. He remembered Jo's admission to working with a politician over a year ago. He had no doubt that this was whom she was talking about. "Which one?" Andre asked.

"I'm still working on getting a name. The attorneys are running interference."

"That's one in a hundred," Daniel said.

"Although when this gag order ends, all bets are off. For the last few months everyone's sitting on a powder keg."

"A powder keg, how so?" Andre asked.

"Whatever happened, whatever she did, whatever she knows she could conceivably write an exposé and basically bring down somebody's house of cards."

"Not if she has no evidence to back up her claims. The courts took her files, right?" Daniel said.

"Not necessarily, Dad," Andre injected. "Being PR I know that public opinion is far more damaging to companies and careers than anything else. Evidence is rarely needed."

"Andre's right, if this senator is important enough then it doesn't matter about legitimate proof, the damage will be done. You can bet there's a politician out there somewhere counting the days. Rumor has it that Ms. Butler's business partner and attorney, Pamela Gibson, Lydia Gibson's daughter, has been inundated with publishing offers for months. The media smells blood; they just don't know whose it is, yet."

"Why didn't any of this come up before?" Daniel asked.

"Although the gag order was holding tight, the unnamed senator is quietly pushing for some kind of a nondisclosure national security letter to keep Ms. Butler legally quiet, but that request doesn't look as if it will succeed. Whatever she knows is of a personal nature and not of national security interest."

"Find out which senator," Andre said.

"I'm already on it," Ben said. "You also should know that there's a tabloid newspaper offering her twenty-five thousand dollars for the exclusive article, sight unseen."

"This doesn't sound right," Andre muttered. "There's something wrong."

"You're damned right there's something wrong," Daniel said gruffly. "We let this woman into the family home and we're giving her access to our past. Can you imagine the damage she can cause? No wonder she refused to leave. She sees another meal ticket."

"No, I don't buy it," Andre said, "I know her."

"Come on, Andre, this isn't like you. Since when do you turn against the family?"

"I'm not turning against the family. It just doesn't make sense."

"Fine, then tell me, why else is she still there? Why be so adamant about staying? It can't be just to write a bio. She's here to get information to blackmail us. Can you imagine how much the other tabloids would counteroffer?"

"Maybe, maybe not," Ben said.

"Obviously she has more than a passing interest in the

Buchanan family. Fraud, blackmail, looks like she intends to do the same thing to us," Daniel said. "She had an affair with a senator to further her career."

"We don't know that, Dad. There's no evidence to support any of this," Andre said defensively. "We need more information before jumping to conclusions."

"It's feasible, that's all the conclusion I need. I for one don't intend to sit around and wait for her to do her damage. I talked to your grandfather, but he's still adamant about her being there. He's enamored with the woman, but this will change his mind."

"One more thing," Ben began. "I don't know how relevant it is at this point, but while in college Joanna Butler did a few freelance articles for a tabloid magazine."

"There you have it, she's a plant," Daniel said immediately. "This is exactly what I was afraid of. We hit the news with our new energy program one day and she hits it with her exposé on us the next. We'll be ruined."

"No, she's not a tabloid plant," Andre said.

"This is already too far out of hand. Have you tried offering her money?"

"She wouldn't take it."

"How do you know?"

"Trust me, I know."

"Then what else can we do? This distracting plan of yours just isn't working fast enough."

"It's working," Andre affirmed.

"It had better work," Daniel warned.

"I need to know what happened. I want to see those court transcripts," Andre insisted.

"Impossible at the moment, all the records have been sealed. Whatever happened, it must be something pretty serious or pretty embarrassing, because nobody's talking. I'm working a contact to perhaps get a look, but it's gonna take time and money. The sensitivity of the parties involved is being protected more than usual," Ben said.

"Okay, you do what you need to do," Daniel said. "Nothing illegal and keep the family name out of it."

"Understood," Ben said readily. "I e-mailed everything to your BlackBerry. You should have it by now."

"You what?" Andre asked as his heart slammed hard against his chest. Ben had done the usual, e-mailed everything to his BlackBerry. It was standard procedure for him to do that. But what was sent to his BlackBerry would also be sent to his home computer.

"I e-mailed everything to your BlackBerry," Ben repeated.

Andre felt ill. "I have to go," he said quickly.

"Andre, before you go," Daniel said. "Your cell was off last night. I left you a message this morning. Your cousin needs you in Los Angeles as soon as possible. In the meantime, do what you do best, take her down now."

It was the call to arms that he oftentimes relished. Like his great-grandfather, he had a talent for manipulation. But this time the vile words only echoed in his ears. His father was demanding the impossible. Love had changed that. Love had changed him. "I'll call you later." He disconnected quickly and looked around, feeling the cold morning air chill his lungs. His heart was beating fast and his breathing was labored. Unfortunately neither had anything to do with his run. Andre turned and ran back to the house. Thoughts raced through his mind as fast as he ran.

Was she, as his father suggested, in search of another big pay day? He didn't believe it. She'd mentioned that she'd worked for a politician. She didn't lie exactly, but she didn't tell the truth, at least not all of it. Entering the house, he headed straight to his office. He looked down at the monitor seeing the message Ben had sent. He clicked the attachments and a new screen popped up. Everything was there, including scanned documents. He saved the file.

He sat back and wondered what happened. Did she have an affair then try to blackmail a senator? If it were true then she'd played him. But still he knew that he couldn't do this, not to the woman he loved. At that moment he noticed the message light blinking on his machine. He pushed the button.

"Andre, your cell phone is off. Call me as soon as you can. Ben got some new information on Joanna Butler. Looks like you were right not to trust her. She's going to be a bigger problem than we anticipated. Whatever you're doing to get rid of her do it faster. Also, I just got off the phone with your cousin. He needs you in Los Angeles again. So bribe her, charm her, screw her, whatever it takes, whatever your plan—just get her away from here. Your grandfather doesn't need this distraction and neither do we. I don't need to tell you how important this new venture is."

Andre pressed the erase button. His father's message, in its usual bluntness, was crystal clear. He was right, he knew he needed to finish this now. But not in the way he expected. He left the office to go to Jo. As soon as he got to the front stairs he saw her coming down, her coat over her arm. "We need to talk," he said.

"You're back early. When'd you get in?" she asked, the coolness in her tone evident.

Andre watched as she walked down the remaining steps. "A few minutes ago. I see you're dressed. You're leaving?"

"Do you know when Jacob is coming back?" she asked.

"No," he said watching her closely, trying to figure out if she knew what he was doing and had been playing him from the beginning. She walked over and glanced out the front window. "Jo, I will protect my family," he said.

She turned back to face him. "Are we back to that again?"

"We never left it," he said solemnly.

"Obviously," she said, matching his coldness. "So I gather the plan was to make me fall for you, then what? I'd be so in love that I'd just walk away from the job? And all this between us was just a game to keep me distracted and away from my job and Jacob until you got something on me?" He didn't respond. She smiled and shook her head. "Thanks, I guess I should feel honored. I had the undivided attention of Andre Buchanan for four whole days. I'm sure very few women can say that." He still didn't respond. "What is it that's so crucial that you'd go to these lengths to hide it? There's no family secret that important. Was it that your great-grandfather was a bootlegger, he smuggled guns, what?" She moved to the window and looked out.

"You wrote for a tabloid magazine?"

"Yes, ten years ago," she said without turning around.

"Do you still freelance for them?"

"No," she said flatly.

"Why don't you tell me about your last client," he asked.

"What do you want to know?" she asked turning back to him.

"I want to know what happened, what you did."

"I'm a ghost writer, I wrote."

"What exactly did you write?" he asked coolly.

"Articles, press releases, blog notes, things like that."

"Anything else?"

"Look," she said, pointedly turning to him, "if you want to ask me something I suggest you man up and do it."

"Tell me about the lawsuit," he said, moving to stand in front of her.

"No," she said blankly, looking up at him.

He was surprised to hear her definitive answer. "No, that's it? No reason, no added remarks, just no?"

"You want more, fine. No comment," she said smartly.

"I need to know, Jo. Tell me about the senator," he said. "Did you sleep with him to further your career?"

She looked at him, surprised by the question. "I don't know how you found out about that since the proceedings are sealed and a gag order was issued, but I suggest whoever gave you the initial information can fill you in with the rest. So go back and ask them."

"What am I supposed to believe?" he asked, reaching out to take her hand.

"Believe whatever you want," she said, stepping away before he could touch her.

"I guess that's my answer. Does my grandfather know about you and what happened with the senator?"

"Are you unfamiliar with the term gag order?"

"So he doesn't," Andre said. She didn't reply. A car horn blew outside. It drew both their attention for a few seconds. "Tell me, Jo, is this job that important that you would jeopardize us?"

She looked at him fiercely. "There is no us," she said coldly. He actually looked hurt by her biting words. "How far were you going to take this? When were you going to tell me that you were just using me?" She spoke haltingly as her voice broke with emotion.

"What are you talking about?" he asked.

She looked at him in astonishment. Apparently he intended to play this until the end. "I'm talking about your father on the answering machine and I'm talking about my life on the screen. I'm talking about your plan to manipulate me. Well, congratulations, it worked." She spun around quickly and headed to the door.

He hurried after her, stopping her as she opened the

door. He grabbed her waist and drew her close to his body. "Jo, that's not how it is now. I love you. All that other stuff doesn't matter."

"It does to me." The car horn beeped again, this time more insistently. She stepped away from him and opened the door.

"Where are you going?" he asked quickly.

"Back to work. I have a job to finish."

"And if my grandfather doesn't want you?"

"He will," she tossed over her shoulder as she opened the front door and got into the cab. It drove off.

Chapter 16

The cab drove off just as Andre's XF Jaguar pulled up. If their timing was for appearance's sake, it was nearly perfect. Neither spoke as they walked up the front steps, Jo first, Andre following. When they got to the top step Andre broke the silence. "You didn't answer my question."

"I answered you. You just didn't like the answer."

"Is that all you're going to say?"

She turned quickly to face him. He was closer than she anticipated. Her breath caught and her heart rate soared as she glared into his eyes. "Can't you just trust me?"

"How can I?"

"So much for your love, I guess," she said.

"And that's just it, I do still love you," he said.

"Oh please, don't insult me," she said. "I know it was all part of some plan to manipulate me. You won. You got what you wanted—for me to leave the house. I can finish your grandfather's job someplace else."

"I don't get it, I don't get you. After everything's that's happened, why is it still so important to do this? How will it benefit you in the end? Is someone paying you to do this to us?"

"It's important because I gave my word and for some people that's enough. You know what? You're too used to liars, backstabbing and deceit. Now you see it everywhere, but strangely enough there are some honest hard-working people out here who just want to do the right thing. That's the difference between you and me, when I give my word I keep it. I mean it. When I said that I love you, I meant it."

"I did too."

She opened her mouth to answer, but decided on a better response. Apparently he wasn't going to let it go, so she was going to show him what he lost. Without a second thought she reached up and kissed him passionately. He grabbed her instantly, holding her tight against his body. Want and desire was back as their mouths devoured each other and their tongues moved in synchronized perfection. They got lost in the kiss. When it ended she looked away breathless. "That's what love feels like."

To their surprise Jacob opened the door smiling happily. "Well now, it's good to see you two haven't killed each other."

Jo's jaw dropped open. Seeing Jacob standing there smiling officially made the situation a complete embarrassment. He didn't react or mention what he had to have witnessed, but the gleam of knowing was certainly in his eyes. "Not yet, but almost," Jo said, then smiling tightly she tried to project some semblance of professionalism. "Jacob, it's good to see you."

"Don't just stand out there like strangers, come in, come in," Jacob said, opening the door wider for them to enter. "I wondered what happened to you two, glad to see everything's okay."

"Hello, Grandfather, welcome back. How was Anchorage?"

Jacob shook Andre's hand then hugged him. "We'll talk about that in a few minutes."

"When did you get in?" Jo asked, hoping it wasn't the night before.

"Last night," Jacob said.

Jo looked at Andre. His cocky half smile said it all. Whatever Jacob suspected of them was right there on Andre's face. There was no doubt Jacob knew that they spent the night together. "Jacob, we need to talk," she said.

"We will, later this afternoon. Right now I need to speak with my grandson here."

Jo nodded and half smiled. "Sure, of course, I'll be upstairs working." She started past him.

"Jo, were you able to get much done on the bio?"

"Yes, as a matter of fact I did," Jo said, turning back to face him. "I reviewed all the previous notes and made some of my own. I think it's a great start and a spellbinding story. But we'll discuss all that when we talk later."

"Excellent."

Both men watched as Jo went upstairs. When she got to the top and turned in the direction of her room, Jacob turned to Andre. "Come, let's get some air."

Andre followed his grandfather outside onto the deck. He knew the look in his eye. He'd seen it a hundred times. At barely five foot nine and one hundred and sixty pounds, his grandfather might appear to be a frail old man to most, but Andre knew better. Jacob Buchanan didn't still actually run the company, but he did run the family. They might not agree with his process or his methods, but there was never any denying the outcome. Jacob always came out on top. This family knew too well the power he still wielded.

Jacob walked outside to the cast-iron railing and looked

out at the view. It was spectacular. The mountains crested against the sky and a soft halo of clouds sat on top. A mass of green stretched out as far as the eye could see. He stood a moment just looking out, admiring the life he made. "I sometimes forget just how invigorating this view can be. It makes you feel alive, like you could conquer the universe."

Andre stood, leaning his back on the rail. He turned and looked out at the beauty. "Yes, it is awesome, but I know you didn't bring me out here to admire the view."

"Do you want to tell me what's going on? What you're up to?" Jacob asked plainly.

"I don't know what you mean," Andre said.

"Like hell you don't. I have high blood pressure, a touch of arthritis in my joints, a wicked backache when it rains, but with all that, I'm no doddering old fool. I know when something's going on in my house. Don't play games with me. Remember, I taught you the games. Now one more time, you want to tell me what's going on here?"

Of course Andre knew exactly what his grandfather was talking about. He had to have seen the kiss on the front porch. "Granddad, what you saw earlier was incidental. It's between Jo and me. I'm not discussing my personal life with you."

"If it encroaches on my plans you will."

Andre knew there was no getting around this conversation. "I know you like her and you want her around to help you with this bio, but she needs to leave now. We can't afford to have her here, she can't be trusted." He said the words, and each one seemed to pierce his heart as he spoke.

"And you know this how?" Jacob asked.

"There are things you don't know about her, potentially damaging things that could affect this company and this family."

"Such as?" Jacob offered.

"Such as, she worked with a tabloid magazine."

"I know, they bought a few of her articles years ago."

"She's currently in litigation with a U.S. senator for ethics violations, fraud and blackmail. If any one of these accusations is true, it makes her more dangerous to us than any of the others put together. I don't know the particulars, but whatever they are we don't need her spotlight on us right now."

"Did she tell you all this?"

"No. I had Ben check her out."

"Why not just ask her?"

"I did. She refused to answer my questions."

"Maybe you asked her the wrong questions."

"Granddad, I get that you like her. She's a very attractive, intelligent and desirable woman. Any man would be crazy not to want her in his life, but you can't trust her."

"Of course I can," Jacob said, "and you're right, I do like her, always have. I think you like her too."

"Whether I like her or not isn't the point. This has nothing to do with me anymore. It's about the family."

"Actually, now I think it does have to do with you." Jacob chuckled, sensing something very different about Andre. "Oh, it started out with you protecting my interests, but somewhere in the past few days things changed for you, didn't they?" Andre went silent. "No need to answer. I can see it as plain as day. You're in love with her."

"Yes, I love her. But I can control how I feel. Don't mistake that kiss you saw earlier. I can and will separate business from pleasure."

Jacob's smile broadened as he shook his head. "No you can't, at least not this time. She got to you. It's in your eyes and all over your face. You're in love with her. And by the look on her face I'd say there was more than an excellent chance that she's in love with you too."

Andre didn't answer right away. He didn't want any of

what his grandfather was saying to be true. But he knew that it was.

"There's nothing wrong with finding that one special woman and giving your life to her. I found mine years ago. I wouldn't trade my life with your grandmother for anything in the world."

"Granddad, whatever my feelings are is beside the point. I have an obligation to this family. I turned my back on that once before for love and I have no intention of doing it again."

"Andre, son, you have an obligation to yourself. Jo is not that other woman."

"It doesn't matter."

"It does when it feels so right."

"Granddad, this is business, not personal."

"Wrong, it's always personal when it comes to my family."

"Granddad…" Andre began, but stopped when Jacob held his hand up.

"Trust me. She has her reasons for being here, for doing what she's doing. So leave it alone for now."

"You don't know her history."

"What makes you think I don't?" Jacob asked.

Andre turned to his grandfather, seeing the bright, knowing sparkle in his eye. "You know, don't you," he said. Jacob didn't answer. "Who told you? Ben?"

"I don't need a private investigator to get information. She didn't change, just the things you think you know about her have," Jacob said.

"And that's enough for me," Andre said.

"Is it?" Jacob asked.

"I'm trying to protect you."

"I think you're trying to protect yourself," Jacob said.

Andre didn't answer, instead he just looked off into the distance. He knew in his heart that this was a no-win situation for him. If he protected his family he'd risk losing the woman he loved.

"Son, don't let one bad past experience with a woman cloud your future. You of all people know the tricks of smoke and mirrors. Manipulation is a game you play very well, but sometimes you need to stop thinking with your head and start feeling with your heart. Not everyone is out to destroy the Buchanan family."

Andre needed distance. "But then again, some are," he said plainly. "Tell me something, what made you first hire her?"

"I didn't."

"What do you mean you didn't?" he asked turning around. "Who did?"

Jacob smiled. "See, there's more to this than meets the eye. Let it go for now."

Andre nodded. "Los Angeles, New York then Washington. I'm leaving in twenty minutes, so let's talk about business."

Slamming and breaking things wasn't her style, but right now she felt as if she could tear down the entire house with her bare hands. The steely control of her emotions had long since waned and she wanted to scream. Instead, she paced, which was her preferred choice of anger release. Back and forth she marched, turning tight corners and mumbling to herself. "This can't be happening. This can't be happening." Finally she plopped down in the chair, opened her laptop and started working.

It wasn't until her charging cell phone rang did she realize that she'd been working steadily for the last two and a half hours. She grabbed her cell and looked at the caller ID. It was Pam. She answered, "Hey."

"Don't hey me all nonchalant, where have you been? I've been calling you for the last two days. Is everything okay?"

"Don't ask," Jo said.

"Oh no, what happened?"

"Andre Buchanan happened."

"You said you could handle him."

"That was before," Jo said stalking across the room and slamming into the padded chair by the window.

"What do you mean before, before what?" Pamela asked.

"Before everything." Jo broke down and told Pamela about Andre and the past few days together. She started with the kiss in the library the first night and ended with the night they spent together and the argument afterward.

"Jo, have you gone insane?"

"Probably," Jo said, holding back the tears.

"You're incredible. You go months and months without a man in your life. You ignore or shoot down perfectly nice guys after one date. And then you do this, have a torrid affair and fall in love with Andre Buchanan of all people in a matter of days. The man specializes in deception, manipulation and breaking hearts. I told you that. He distracted you from your work, didn't he? What were you thinking?"

"Again, don't ask."

"Of all the men to get involved with, Andre Buchanan is notorious for his cold-hearted relationships."

"His reputation is extremely well-deserved." She paused a few seconds. "I don't know what to do."

"There's nothing you can do. You feel how you feel."

"How can I continue to work with Jacob after everything that's happened? I can't. I need to leave. I can finish this at home."

"Are you going to be okay?"

"I'm a survivor, you know that. I'll be fine."

"Jo, everything will work out."

"I'll call you later." She hung up then went back to work. An hour later the phone on the desk rang. She saved her document then picked it up. It was Bane. He called to tell her that lunch would be served in fifteen minutes. She quickly read over the last page of her document, made changes, and then saved it again. She washed her hands and face then went downstairs. It was time to face the music.

She met Jacob in the dining room. He was standing at the large bay window staring out. She stood in the doorway for a few seconds before entering, making sure Andre wasn't still there. He wasn't. She focused her attention back on Jacob. He seemed pensive and distracted. "You look deep in thought," she said, walking over to stand beside him at the window.

He turned smiling. "Hello, Jo, yes, I suppose I am."

Neither spoke as she looked out at the panoramic view. "It's so peaceful and beautiful here."

"Yes it is. It's everything my father worked for. It's everything I worked for. I spent so many hours focusing on getting it all, having it all, keeping it with me. I just assumed it would make me happy in the end." He shook his head sadly. "I wasted so much time focusing on the wrong things."

"We all do," she commiserated, "but I think that's what allows us to change and learn from our mistakes. Although sometimes it's too late."

"And other times it's not." Jacob turned to her and smiled. "I have a feeling we're talking about two different things," he said, "or maybe not."

"We probably are. Jacob, we need to talk about the memoir," she began.

"Yes, I believe we do. I have some wonderful new ideas to discuss with you," he said excitedly.

"Good, great, I can't wait to hear them."

"Ah," he interrupted again, seeing that lunch was being

brought into the dining room. "Excellent, lunch is here. Come, sit. We'll discuss this over lunch." They walked to the table and sat down.

Jo noticed that Andre still hadn't appeared. "Isn't Andre eating with us?"

"No, Andre has business to attend to. He'll be away for the next few days."

"Oh, I see," she said, trying not to sound as disappointed as she was. She wanted him gone and now he was. It was supposed to be a good thing, so why was she feeling so empty? Catching herself, she smiled pleasantly, hoping Jacob would buy the charade, but it was obvious he didn't.

"I hope you got some rest, because we still have a lot of work to do," he said.

"Yes, I did and work is exactly what I need to talk to you about. With all the information I have now, I'm sure I can finish this up on my own. I've gone through and organized all the boxes, listened to the tapes you recorded and read all the notes. I don't need to be here on site any longer."

"I thought you always stayed with the client until the end to complete the project."

"I do usually, but I think for all concerned it would be best for me to finish this on my own. My flight leaves tomorrow morning."

"No, that won't do," he said decisively.

"Jacob, it wasn't a request, it was fact. I'm leaving."

Jacob put his fork down and looked at her, sighing heavily. "This is about Andre," he said.

She considered denying it, but she knew he'd see through her. "Yes, in part, but it's more about me. I made a mistake coming here. I know I gave my word to finish what was started, but I can't, at least not here."

"Allow me to change your mind."

"I don't think that's possible."

"Anything's possible. I recently came across some old journals that belonged to my father. I think you'll find them very revealing."

"I've already gone through the boxes you left me. Some of the information was priceless and some was a bit surprising."

"Yes, the Buchanan history is varied. But I think you'll find these journals particularly of interest. They tell about his journey from New Orleans to New York to here. Trust me when I say these journals will highlight the project. But they are not to leave this house."

Jo was hesitant. She wanted out as soon as possible, but she also wanted the job done right. And journals from Louis Buchanan might be exactly what she was looking for. "Okay, I'll stay a few more days."

"Excellent," Jacob said, raising his glass to her.

"Jacob, I know quite a bit about you and your father since the book was originally centered on your past and present. I know a little about other members of the family, but not a lot about your wife. Tell me about you and Olivia."

Jacob stared across the table to the empty chair and smiled wistfully. He seemed to drift off into his own world. "Olivia was a dream, every man's fantasy. She was beautiful, smart, funny and strong-willed. She had a spirit that was unstoppable." He looked over and saw Jo smile. "She was special, very special. I didn't appreciate that when I had her with me. Work and other foolish distractions were too important at the time. If I could have the time back to be with her…" He paused and looked away before continuing. "I knew the instant I saw her that I wanted her. It was love at first sight. She was talking to a friend and I walked right up and introduced myself. I knew right then that she was going to be my wife."

"You knew just like that," Jo stated. He nodded. "Did she know who you were?"

"You mean the great Louis Buchanan's son?" he asked. She nodded. "No, we met in France, a world away from Alaska."

"Wow, in France, she didn't tell me that."

"Ah see, there's a lot she didn't tell you, but that's why you're here now. It's my turn to finish what she started. I just wish she would have told me what she was doing at the time."

"She told me that she wanted it to be a surprise. Something for you to have when she was gone," Jo's voice trailed to a whisper as she looked cautiously at Jacob.

He smiled. His reaction was placid. "She never told me she was so sick. I would have never left her side had I known."

"I think that's why she didn't tell you. She knew how much you loved your work. We talked about it all the time. Our conversations and interviews over the phone would last for hours. Then when we met in person we talked for three days and three nights. That's why the project was nearly complete when you finally called me."

"Where did you meet in person, here?"

"No. Olivia came to visit me in New Jersey. Obviously I never have clients come to me, but she wanted to meet there. She was a remarkable woman."

"Indeed she was. That's why I intend to finish what the two of you started. When I found her notes I was furious. I have to admit, I would never have agreed to this project when you began two years ago, but now I think it's time."

"I called one day and was told that she passed. I stopped working on it. She once told me that if anything happened to her she wanted me to put it away until you called."

"That sounds just like her. She knew I'd find her papers and call you."

"I'm glad you did," Jo said. "I'm sure she'd be happy too."

"I promised her I'd finish this and we will."

"Yes, we will," Jo agreed happily.

"Good, so no more of this nonsense about leaving. I have a few more boxes I'd like you to see." They finished lunch and then moved to the library. They continued talking while going through the boxes of letters, photos and memories.

"You've accomplished so much. You're a true visionary."

He chuckled. "I've been called a lot of things. Visionary is certainly one of the most pleasant. Thank you. That's why I've decided that I want this memoir to be published."

"That wasn't the original agreement I had with Olivia. The surprise anniversary gift she commissioned was just for a personal biography. Are you sure?"

"Yes. It's time the rest of the world knew the truth and it's time the Buchanan family faced the past. There's no such thing as honest wealth. It all begins somewhere. When this is complete the events of our family history will seem like fabled literature, but I assure you it's quite true. I know this because it's my family and the history of my family."

"Why are you doing this?"

He sighed wearily and began. "I suppose the uncertainty of life's vicissitudes has brought me to this. The history is firsthand in most cases with some relayed from my father. The particulars are in these journals." He looked down and tapped them gently. "This is the beginning. It's been hidden away for over a century. This is the proverbial closet of skeletons. In here is shame, deceit, death, theft, lies and betrayal. There are no excuses, except that this was a new land and lawlessness prevailed."

"Jacob, you must be mistaken. I've researched and read dozens of documents. Nothing I've read or seen even comes close to anything like that about your family."

"Man records his history as he sees fit. It's predicated on many things. There's always another side to the truth."

"What's the other side of the Buchanan truth?"

"My father was born Thaddeus Boles in 1863, the year the Emancipation Proclamation was signed. He was a Virginia slave. After the emancipation he and his mother continued on at the plantation. At age sixteen Thaddeus ran away. He got as far as the Maryland coast. There he got an apprenticeship position with an engineer named Buchanan building homes on the Potomac. He was indentured."

"A black man as an indentured servant in the south, how was that even possible?"

"Thaddeus was passing. His mother was a house slave and his father, Louis Boles, my grandfather, was the plantation owner. Everyone assumed he was a white man. He didn't correct their misconception. He passed for years after that. There was a fire in one of the Buchanan structures. His mentor, the engineer, was killed and it was presumed he was too. But he survived. So he killed himself off and Louis Buchanan was born. He moved to New York and worked as an office clerk for a rich immigrant banker. He befriended the owner's only son, a spoiled spendthrift with wild dreams of making his own fortune out west.

"In 1885 he partnered with the banker's son, Alden van Rotmensen, and went west to search for gold in California. In 1899 they headed north just as the Klondike gold rush had started. He was thirty-six years old. The two-man expedition was sponsored by Alden's rich parents. They had no other family and no other children and they doted on him.

"The two men mined gold with moderate success. But the first winter here in Alaska Alden died, probably of pneumonia. Nobody really knows. It's also possible that Louis killed him. But as I said, nobody knows. By now

Louis had become a wealthy man financed by his partner's family, who had no idea that their son was dead.

"There was a letter from Alden's parents begging him to return home to New York. They were both gravely ill and didn't expect to live long. They wanted Alden to take over the business. The next letter was from the parents' solicitors. They were both dead and their holdings were being transferred to him. By now Louis had stopped mining gold and was supplying the miners. He made a fortune, enough to own the local bank and a few more prominent businesses.

"The solicitor arrived with the transferred money. He found out that Alden had been dead for years. So Louis allegedly bribed him. With Alden not having any siblings and both the van Rotmensens being only children there was no one left. No descendents, no family, no one to claim the estate. The solicitor transferred the money to Louis, but never made it back to New York. He ran afoul with undesirables in a crooked card game. There is no record of him after that.

"Louis went on to practically own the town and everything in it. By unsavory means he took by force, bribed, conned and swindled his way to success. At age seventy he married a young African-American woman. It was said he always favored black women. Of course the town was in an uproar over this, but since he owned most of it, it didn't much matter. He was a very powerful man and people feared him and his methods. He was the most powerful African-American man in Alaska that no one knew was black.

"By the time I was born in 1933, the mining company had expanded to other minerals. In 1966, it converted solely to oil exploration. All records regarding Louis's past are long gone by way of fires, poor record keeping and just plain destroyed over time. There's nothing left except me and the truth."

"That's an amazing story," she said when he finished his drink.

"It is indeed." He looked down at the journal. "I don't really know what's in these anymore. Papers, photos, documents and deeds I don't know. I haven't dared open them in decades, they hold too many memories that I didn't care to relive. Here, take them." He handed her several old, roughly bound ledgers. "The beginning is here. Write what you will. I'll be in Anchorage for the next few days." He stood and walked to the door.

"Jacob," she called out. He stopped and turned. "About the kiss you saw between Andre and me, it's not what you think."

"I don't know about that," he said, smiling happily. "What I think is that the two of you shared a special time together." Jo looked away. "Oh don't try to deny it. I was young too, a long, long time ago. But it seems that for some reason you're both too stubborn to enjoy the journey. Trust me when I say that love is a fleeting and precious gift. Treasure it before it's too late. Love is the here and now, don't throw it away for later. My grandson loves you and it appears that you love him, just as I loved my Olivia. Our romance was just as swift and sure. Give him time. We Buchanan men take a while, but always come to our senses in the end. Now you get to work, I've got to get back to Anchorage for a while. You'll have the whole house to yourself."

Jo watched as he turned and left the room. She considered his last remark about Andre then decided not to think about it. It was a nice sentiment, but it was too late now. In truth she just needed to answer one very simple question. What do you do when trust is gone? The answer was harsh, but simple. It's what she'd always done. You get back to your life with a vengeance.

She opened the first ledger he'd given her and flipped through the pages. There was a crackling sound as some were brittle and nearly crumbled on the edges. She carefully turned to the first page and read the date.

I was born Thaddeus Boles. It was 1863, the beginning.

Chapter 17

Of course she'd ended relationships before. It was easy enough each time since she never opened her heart in the first place. She'd learned long ago that opening her heart meant hurt and pain. It wasn't that she was cold or callous. It was that she'd seen it too many times in foster care, parents in it only for the money, kids being placed and displaced every few months. It was a hard lesson that she learned well. Then as an adult, she witnessed men who seemed to break hearts for sport. So when it came to her heart, she protected it fiercely. But this time was different. This time she let Andre in. And she had gotten hurt.

The focused vengeance of continuous work lasted the next five days. The house was empty, so Jo stayed at Jacob's insistence and worked on the manuscript nonstop. She took over the library, spread out her materials and worked feverishly. It was hard, but she focused, concentrated and did it. Jacob called every evening with answers to questions she posted earlier that day. She went through every piece of data he supplied. But it was Louis's journals that provided the most interesting data.

She read the journals a few dozen times. Each time she read them, she learned something more incriminating than before. The humble beginnings everyone knew to be true about the wealthy Buchanan family weren't all that humble. Reading the journals changed everything she thought she knew. Jacob was right. Louis Buchanan was a liar, a thief, a con man and a crook. He was the deep dark secret the Buchanans wanted to protect for good reason.

But surely all the good the Buchanans have done over the decades had to make up for sins of the past. Their philanthropic and humanitarian causes were legendary. The Buchanan Foundation, headed at one time by Olivia, was universal in its charitable gifts. They sponsored generous scholarships, awarded grants, and promoted the value of education with words, works and millions of dollars.

Jo continued working day and night and she was exhausted, but she wanted to see this through. It wasn't unusual for her to wake up on the library sofa having fallen asleep from sheer exhaustion. After a particularly long night she stayed up all the next day and that evening reached an astounding conclusion. She was done. She stared at the monitor for a few minutes, stunned by the realization of all her hard work both past and present. Afterward she saved the document and sat back completely numb. She stared blankly at the monitor looking at the completed work. It was done. She was finished.

There was only one last thing to do. She wrote a brief e-mail, attached the file and sent it to Jacob. After a quick shower and snack, her cell rang. She checked the ID and answered. It was Jacob with his usual evening check-in phone call.

"Hi, Jacob, it's finished. I just sent you the file."

"Excellent. What do you think of it?"

"Truthfully, I think it's some of my best work. The family history is so unique and profound that the images leap right off the page. It's heartwarming and tragic. I think anyone reading this will recognize the power of the American dream and the courage and valor of the men who achieve it."

"I hope you didn't exaggerate too much."

"I write the facts. I always do. But the facts are always surrounded by the historical truth of the times. Also, I hope you don't mind, but I used one of your father's journal entries as the prologue. It seemed fitting."

"Thank you, I'm grateful for all your patience and dedication. I know it was difficult and trying at times. Olivia would be delighted."

"You're welcome. And thank you again for the opportunity to work with you. It was very special. I made travel arrangements, and my flight leaves tomorrow morning so I guess this is goodbye. I'll leave a hard copy here waiting for you."

"No, I have a better idea. Why not deliver it in person?"

"Sure, where are you?"

"Bane will come and get you tomorrow morning."

"Okay, see you soon."

Jo hung up. Next she made a quick call to put her travel plans on hold. Her body was drained. She relaxed with the intention of resting her eyes just for a moment. Having not slept much in the past few nights, her eyes grew heavy and soon she'd fallen asleep.

The dream was simple. It was the same dream she'd had all week, with slight variations. She was looking for Andre and found him in his bathroom. He was in the large tub filled with warm water and surrounded by bubbles. Candles glowed everywhere and soft music played in the background. She walked in. He saw her and motioned for her to join him. She did. Relaxed back in his embrace she closed her eyes, feeling the sensation of his body holding her. They were surrounded and covered with iridescent bubbles.

Then the bathroom disappeared and they were suddenly outside, still in a tub but in the middle of winter. They were on the tiny patch of land he took her to and there was snow all around them, but the steaming hot water kept them cocooned in warmth.

His hands came to her shoulders and began massaging her gently. She sighed as her head rolled back and all her stress and tension washed away. He drizzled warm water onto her breasts as her nipples hardened. He kissed and nibbled her neck as he tweaked each one. She gasped, feeling sweet sensation. From her shoulders his hands drifted lower to her breasts, to her stomach and then to her hips. He pulled her body onto his and began touching her everywhere. There was no end to his touch.

She felt his mouth, his tongue and his hands. He was in front of her, behind her, beneath her and on top of her all at the same time. Her mind was dizzy with ecstasy as water rippled and a hot mist rose up around them. Everything seemed lighter than air, including them as they floated while making love. The image of his body began to fade. She tried to hold on, but he slowly slipped from her grasp until finally he was nothing more than a mist.

Slowly she opened her eyes. It was morning and she'd been dreaming. She was in Jacob's library with piles of books and boxes all around her. She sat up and looked around. She was alone and her muted cell was humming and vibrating. She answered sleepily.

"We have a problem," Pam said immediately. "You're in the newspaper, named by Senator Lewis on her divorce. Apparently the gag order isn't as final as we thought."

"What?"

"The judge is furious and I'm headed over there now. Apparently someone leaked that Lewis's husband was having an affair. Details are sketchy, but your name came up."

"Are you serious? This is a disaster. Who would do something like this?"

"One guess, does the name Andre Buchanan sound familiar?"

"No, Andre wouldn't do this to me."

"Are you sure? The man is a media master. He plays by his own rules when it comes to protecting his family. If he sees you and this bio as a threat he will end it and if that means discrediting you before the fact, he will."

"No, I don't believe it."

"Who else then? The senator or her husband? No, there's no way either of them would talk to the media about this. It's her career on the line and his reputation."

Jo's shoulders slumped. Pamela was right, who else had the savvy, the means and the motive to leak this information? It was revenge, plain and simple. "It doesn't matter now anyway, I just finished the manuscript and sent it to Jacob. If he wants to have it published, then it's on him. I'm done. I'll just move on to the next job."

"About that, I just got off the phone with them. They canceled."

"They canceled me?" Jo asked.

"Don't worry, I'll find something else."

"Actually, I think I'm gonna take a little vacation."

"Are you sure?" Pamela asked.

"Positive. Listen, I have to go."

"Where to?"

"You know what? I have no idea."

Bane called shortly after that to set up a time to pick her up. She dressed and prepared for the meeting, but was sur-

prised when Bane called and asked her to meet him out
back. When the time came she walked around to the back
of the house and waited. A few minutes later she saw a helicopter arrive and land. Bane hopped out and greeted her.
"Are you ready to go?" he asked.

"Are you kidding, in that?" she shouted, over the loud
whirl of the blades and motor.

"Sure, believe me, it's the safest way to travel. There are
no traffic jams, no road rage and no accidents when you
hit a cloud."

"Yeah, but most cars don't fall a hundred feet out of the
air when you run out of gas."

"We work for an energy company, believe me, we have
fuel," he teased as he guided her across the landing pad to
the helicopter. He opened the door and got her settled with
a secured seat belt and a headset. He got in on the other
side and told the pilot to take off.

"Where are we going exactly?" she asked.

"Titan."

An hour and six hundred miles later Jo arrived in Anchorage at Jacob's insistence. He wanted her to see and experience the heart of Titan. He was right, the corporate
headquarters of Titan Energy Corporation in Anchorage
was as impressive as the company itself. It was massive,
spread out over miles and miles. Jo looked down at the
property as the helicopter hovered. She felt her heart skip
a beat. It wasn't because of the ride, but because she knew
she might see Andre again.

"What do you think?" Bane asked through the speaker
in her headset.

"It's massive," she said, "I've never seen anything so
big."

"The offices are over there. There are three corporate
buildings. Each houses a different aspect of the business.

Jacob and most of the Buchanan family are in the executive building over there." He pointed as the helicopter flew over and hovered low.

"Are there oil wells around here?"

"Not in the traditional sense. The oil fields are pipelines that run from up north and to the west. They're also located off the coastlines. You'll see a lot more natural gas lines coming down from the Prudhoe Bay area on the Arctic Ocean."

"I still can't believe we're so close to the Arctic."

"We're still quite a few kilometers south. Okay, ready to head in?" he asked.

"Yes. Thank you so much. The tour was amazing." The helicopter instantly changed directions and headed back toward the three main buildings. It hovered over the smallest building and landed on the roof. As soon as it powered down, Bane removed his headset and helped her with hers. They got out, ducked low and hurried to the building's rooftop exit. Bane swiped a key card and the latch clicked. Inside sat a security guard. He looked up and nodded then checked Bane's ID and signed her in. "Wow. That was really amazing," Jo said.

"Your first helicopter ride?" Bane asked, as the elevator arrived. They got in and Bane used a key and pressed the button.

"Yes."

"You get used to them after awhile. It's the quickest way to get from point A to point B sometimes." The elevator door opened and they stepped out into a busy rush of employees. "Wait here, I'll let Jacob know we've arrived." He came back a few minutes later. "He's not in his office, come on, we'll track him down."

Chapter 18

Five days was a long time to stay away, and it might just as well have been five years. Because it didn't matter how far he went or where he went—Los Angeles, New York or Washington—he couldn't stop thinking about Jo. Andre had gotten into the Anchorage office early and sat at his desk listening to his staff update and address current issues in his absence. They talked, but he barely listened. His focus was shot. It had been for the past week. Then finally he asked them to just take a break and meet with him again later that afternoon. The last of his staff left, closing the door and leaving him alone.

He stood and walked over to his window. From the eighth floor he could see that the extensive view stretched out for miles. His thoughts traveled just as far and wide. He'd made a decision. He loved Jo and if that meant turning his back on his family then so be it, that's what he intended to do. He went back to his desk, picked up the phone and called his father's office. A second later there was knock on his door. "Come," he said, looking up.

His father strolled in happily. "Good, you're back, excellent," Daniel said.

"I was just calling you. We need to talk."

"Yes indeed, we have a few things to discuss before the meeting with the conglomerate tomorrow. This needs to run smoothly. We don't need any last-minute surprises. By the way, nice job on clearing up that writer matter. That could have been a problem."

"What do you mean?"

"Ben sent the newspaper. Didn't you get it?"

"No, what newspaper?" he asked.

"The Washington Post. Check your desk, it came overnight express. I got mine this morning."

Andre rifled through the pile of waiting mail he had yet to go through and found the overnight express envelope from Ben. He opened it and read the notation. The article was straightforward. It alleged that Jo had had an affair with Senator Lewis's husband while in her employ. It listed an anonymous informant as the source.

"Excellent job," Daniel added. "It'll show any other vultures with a mind to take advantage of the Buchanan name just what the consequences will be."

"I didn't do this," Andre said, as his father continued to congratulate him. "This isn't me."

"Of course it is, it has your style written all over it. It gets the point across without directly linking us to the scandal. I think it's a stroke of brilliance."

"That may be, but not this time."

Just then the door opened wide and Jacob marched in obviously furious. "What is this trash?" he asked, angrily. "I specifically instructed you to leave her alone. She didn't deserve this attack."

"He was following my lead on this, Dad," Daniel said instantly. "This was getting out of hand and somebody needed to bring it back under control. You've had your affairs and flings with these women, even before Mom's death, and I've never said a word, but this is over the top. You were giving this woman the keys to our past and sacrificing all our careers."

"This has nothing to do with you," Jacob said.

"It has everything to do with me, with all of us. Do you have any idea what could happen if this thing she's been working on gets out? We could be ruined, everything gone. This way she has no reason to continue plus it gives her and others like her warning not to try anything like this again."

Jacob shook his head. "She's done. She finished it last night and sent it to me. I read it and forwarded it to a publisher friend of mine. They want the full story."

"No, Dad, you didn't, you can't," Daniel said in frustration.

"It's out of my hands, it always was."

"What do you mean, is this woman blackmailing you to do this?" Daniel asked. "If so we can—"

"No," Andre interrupting, drawing both their attention. "It's out of your hands because you never commissioned it or hired her in the first place. Somebody else did. Jo told me that she was already nearly done, but the job was interrupted. It was interrupted because Grandmom is the one who hired her, wasn't she?"

Jacob smiled and nodded. "I was wondering when you were going to figure that out. I expected the realization much sooner. You must have been distracted."

"No one else could have possibly been able to convince you to do this. It had to be her. So that's why she was so adamant about doing this."

Daniel walked over to the sofa and sat down. "Mom did this? Impossible."

"Originally Olivia wanted a book, but I refused. She started it anyway without my knowledge. After she passed I found a letter from her asking that I continue what she and Jo started. I couldn't do it for months. I felt too guilty, too lost. Olivia was my world and I didn't appreciate her and what she gave me until it was too late."

"So what happens now?" Daniel asked. "We need to call a press conference to head this off before the sharks start circling."

"No, what happens now is that you read the manuscript," Jacob said. "You never know, this just might be good for all of us."

"Impossible. How can this be good? You invited this woman into our lives and she's wreaked havoc on all of us," Daniel replied.

"Not all of us," Jacob said, eyeing Andre.

"Andre, we need a press conference. We can jump on Senator Lewis's publicity and say that this woman is trying to do the same thing to us." He jumped up and moved to the desk, grabbing the newspaper and handing it to him. "We can use this, we'll bury her," Daniel said as he marched toward the office door and opened it.

Andre shook his head and leaned back against the front of his desk. "Sorry, Dad, I can't do it."

Daniel spun around. "Excuse me, what did you just say?" He looked at Andre as if he'd suddenly grown two heads.

"You heard me, Dad. I quit."

"What?" Daniel bellowed loud enough to register on a noise decibel scale.

"I quit," Andre said calmly. "You go after Jo and I will quit."

Daniel threw his arms up and walked away. "This is

crazy, first Dad and now you. What's going on? Is everybody losing their minds around this place? She's infected
you too, hasn't she?"

Jacob chuckled and nodded. "It appears that way."

"This is insane," Daniel continued. "What's going on
around here? Has everybody gone crazy? Do you have any
idea what our future will be like?"

Andre smiled. "Yes, as a matter of fact I do. I love her
and if she'll still have me, my future will be with her."

"That's my boy," Jacob said proudly.

Daniel threw his arms up again. "Oh, this is impossible. I'm dealing with craziness here."

"Not craziness, Daniel, love," Jacob added.

"I need to go to her."

"Actually…" Jacob began just as Bane knocked on the
open door. Jo stood beside him looking directly at Andre.
She had heard everything.

"Jacob, your guest has arrived," Bane said.

"Excellent. Come in, welcome to Titan," Jacob said.

Jo walked in cautiously as the three Titan men all stared
at her. The smell of power, money and influence was all
around her. Having heard the bulk of conversation she immediately felt defensive. "Hello," she said awkwardly,
then turned her attention to Jacob, the only Titan smiling,
obviously delighted to see her.

"What are you doing here?" Andre asked.

"I'm delivering the manuscript."

"So this is the woman who would topple us," Daniel
hissed.

"Dad, this is Joanna Butler," Andre said, introducing the
two.

"Do you have any idea what you've done?" he asked
her.

"Do you?" Jo asked him simply enough. Daniel

frowned and seemed about to reply when she cut him off. She walked to him and handed him the manuscript. He took it grudgingly. "I think you should read this and reserve judgment before trashing it. It's not exactly what you might think." She turned to Jacob. "I had a change of heart, I hope you don't mind. The bio reads slightly differently than what we talked about. It's Olivia's original idea. It's what she intended all along."

"And it's brilliant," Jacob said, "I read it last night, couldn't put it down. Thank you, thank you, you've brought my Olivia back to me with this." Jo smiled brightly. It's exactly what she wanted to hear. "Daniel, why don't we go to your office, I'll tell you all about it."

"Dad…" he began.

"Trust me, the truth will be good you, for all of us." The two men left, leaving Jo and Andre alone in his office.

Jo walked over to the large windows and looked out. "Is there any place in this state that doesn't have an incredible view?"

He followed and stood beside her. "I was coming to see you."

She turned quickly. "I know, I heard. I guess I heard everything, more than I should have. I have something for you." She reached into her purse and grabbed a small flash drive. "It's the finished manuscript."

He took the drive from her. "I thought you only delivered your finished work to the client, no one else."

"I thought I'd amend my rule and make an exception this one time. Read it, it's not half bad. Oh, and I found this in one of the ledgers Jacob had me read." She gave him a large envelope. He opened and looked inside pulling out old documents.

"What's all this?"

"There are things in the book that might appear wrong,

criminal even. These documents prove that Louis legally acquired everything he had. Of course we don't know the complete story, but I like to believe that he was a lot like you. Manipulative when necessary, but very honest in the end." He began flipping through the documents. "I'm not an attorney, but it looks to me like Louis and his partner both signed most of these documents."

"Yeah, so?" he asked.

She stood closer beside him. "This is the original partnership contract between Louis Buchanan and Alden van Rotmensen. In most partnership wills of this era it would be clearly outlined that whatever each of the partners attained throughout the active partnership would be equally divided or whatever percentage they deemed. It would also state that in the case that one partner died all owned profits would defer to the surviving partner. But this document isn't exactly written like that. You need your attorneys to check it, but as far as I can see the wording is completely wrong."

"What do you mean, wrong?"

"In essence this document details that, *whatever either partner received during the life of the partnership in total would be divided equally and in the event of death all would go to the surviving partner.* The contract was for the life of the partnership, which was five years. So even though Alden died within the first years of arriving in Alaska, the partnership legally lasted for the next four."

"So you're saying that due to a legal error, everything Louis got was completely legal?"

"It looks that way to me. It may not have been what originally was intended, but when the van Rotmensen family died in New York leaving all their wealth to Alden and he was already dead it was the partnership that was the key. Everything legally reverted to Louis."

"The partnership contract was still in full effect."

She nodded, pulling out another document and handing it to him. "Louis couldn't legally dissolve the partnership for another four years. So the van Rotmensens left everything to a dead man with a live partner. It still comes out the same way. With no van Rotmensen family members to contest, Alden's estate reverted to his partner, Louis."

Andre was amazed. He never knew the whole story. It was common knowledge and the shame within the Buchanan family that Louis swindled and stole from the van Rotmensens, but now it looked as if he never did. "I'll make sure our attorneys take a look at these. But if what you say is correct, then the past doesn't matter. I guess the Buchanan wealth isn't entirely built on theft and corruption after all."

"Well, I don't know about all that. Louis was certainly no saint. The man was outrageous," she said smiling.

"It sounds like he was an arrogant, self-centered jerk and you kind of liked him," he teased, smiling.

"Yeah, how about that," she smiled with him.

"Jo…" he began but his phone rang and there was a knock on his door. He ignored both. "Jo…" The intercom buzzed again. He hurried to his desk and pressed the button on the phone. "Yes," he said impatiently. "Mr. Buchanan, your father needs to see you in his office immediately." He didn't reply. He turned to look at her.

"It's all right, I've got to go anyway. There's a helicopter ride with my name on it." She pointed to the flash drive still in his hand. "Read it. Let me know what you think. I'll see you around," she said, then hurried to leave before her heart wouldn't let her.

Chapter 19

It was time to go. Jo stood out on the deck looking out at the panoramic view one last time. The sky was dark and moody with a billion stars shining bright. It was late, near midnight. Her new travel plans had been confirmed. She was leaving in the morning, but it seemed sleep wasn't coming again tonight and staring out the window just wasn't enough. She got up, dressed and headed downstairs to the deck.

The stillness of the wooded area was almost hypnotic. Shadows played against shadows, turning innocent things into illusive images. Huge soaring birds, ferocious dinosaurs in profile, flying witches, and even a dancing clown. The images distorted and changed as the light winds blew and the leaves adjusted. The channel's dark water glistened in the moonlight, reflecting the stars above, resulting in a spectacular show. There was no way she'd ever forget her time here.

She thought about her future. She had no idea what would happen next. After her conversation with Pamela and hearing that the judge completely dismissed the senator's case, she could go back to writing biographies full time. But the thrill was gone. After the Buchanan family, she couldn't see herself writing about anyone else. It was time for her to find her own life now. What she needed was a sign to point her in a new direction.

The door opened behind her. She turned to see Andre step out on the deck. "You startled me," she said.

"Not my intention." He walked over and stood in front of her. "I thought you'd already gone to bed. Can't sleep?"

"No."

"Ghosts?" he asked.

"No, not this time. I'm looking for a sign."

"What kind of sign?"

"That's just it, I don't know."

They stood eye to eye, motionless. Neither spoke, just stared. Then Andre reached up and gently touched her face. His puzzled expression surprised her. "How do I stop loving you?" he asked her.

She felt tears welling up, but refused to set them free. She stepped away, trying desperately to resist temptation, then turned back to the trees and scenery. "Did you read the manuscript?" she asked, instead of answering his hopeless question.

"I didn't leak the senator's information to the media," he said, standing beside her at the rail. His eyes never left her face.

"I know you didn't," she said. "Pamela called. They found out who broke the gag order."

"Who was it?"

"Senator Lewis's assistant, Eric. He and the senator's husband had been having an affair for years. When the senator's husband tried to break it off because he found someone else, Eric went public."

"How did you…"

"…get in the middle of all this?" she asked. He nodded. "Senator Lewis and I became good friends as I worked on her biography. She knew her husband was having an affair, she just didn't know with whom. I found out and told her. It wasn't what she wanted to hear. She confronted her husband and he lied to her. I became the perfect candidate."

"So you knew about her husband and his lover."

She nodded. "I walked in on them a few days before I was fired. He told the senator that I'd propositioned him and intended to blackmail him if he didn't comply. Eric backed him up in the lie. When I told the truth about what I saw…"

"…she turned on you, fired you and filed suit to keep it quiet."

"Exactly, and everyone believed him. And why not? After all, he's the quintessential, all-American man. He's from a wealthy and powerful family. People choose money and power. But ultimately it was my fault for letting my guard down. I knew better. I got attached and then got hurt. That's just the way it is."

"Not always. My grandfather is having the manuscript published. I suggested he put your name on it along with my grandmother's. He loved the idea."

"I'm honored," she said, "but I'm a ghost writer, that's not really necessary."

"Yes, it is. I read the manuscript," he said.

She turned to him. "What did you think?"

"It's a love story between Jacob and Olivia."

"It always was. It's what Olivia first intended."

"I see your bags are by the front door. You're leaving?"

"Yes, first thing tomorrow morning," she looked away

again. "It's time for me to go. I finished what I was hired to do. It's time to move on."

"Do you have your next job lined up?"

"I did, but it fell through. It's okay. I think I need to take a break for a while anyway. I might check out Montana."

"Why Montana?" he asked

"I don't know, why not?" she said.

"I hear Alaska's nice this time of year," he said, turning toward her.

"Is that right?" she asked, resisting the pull to face him again. He nodded. "I hear it's cold," she said.

"It depends on where you go."

"Where do you suggest?" she asked.

"Juneau, Anchorage, wherever you like," he said.

"Andre…" she began.

"You can't just love me and leave me," he told her, taking her hand and holding it close to his heart. "Stop running away Joanna, you've been doing it all your life. It's time to stop. It's time to stay here with me."

"I can't. I have to go." She pulled away and hurried to the patio door.

"I'll follow you," he said simply. She stopped mid-step. "Montana, New Jersey, Florida, Calcutta, Kalamazoo, wherever you go, I'll follow," he continued as he went to her. He stood behind her and whispered in her ear. "It's time to stop. Don't be afraid, I'm here, I'll always be here."

Jo wrapped her arms around her body, holding herself tight. Tears tipped the corners of her eyes then crawled down her cheeks. "How do I stop running? I don't know how. Losing control, losing myself, I don't want to be like my foster mother. I can't live like that. I love you, I do, but it doesn't matter in the end."

He turned her around to face him. "Sweetheart, love always matters, especially our love. You won't be like your foster mother. There's no way you could lose yourself. You're stronger than that. You always were."

"What about your dad? He's not exactly my biggest fan."

Andre started laughing. "He is now. He's thrilled about the manuscript. After you left he called the publisher and pressured them to get started. They'll be contacting you in a few days. I'm going to spin the book into a campaign push. He wants me to draw up a whole press junket around our past—truth and honesty. Can you imagine that as a political campaign slogan?"

She laughed. "The man is good."

"He's a Buchanan. What about you?"

"What do you mean?" she asked.

"I lost your trust, I know that."

"No, you didn't. You helped me find it again."

"Stay with me, Jo. Be my family, my future, my wife."

"Oh my God," she whispered, weeping instantly. "Oh my God."

"Is that a yes?" he asked, half smiling.

"Oh my God, look at it," she whispered, pointing behind him.

Andre turned around to see the northern lights streaking across the sky. They were dazzling—veiled ribbons of glistening radiance. They shimmered and glowed, dancing across the sky in a multitude of translucent colors—greens, blues, purples and reds, each ribbon more spectacular than the next.

The aurora borealis blazed across the sky for about ten minutes. Both were completely silent and awed by the celestial spectacle. In one seemingly last burst of magnificence, the colors transformed, twisted, whirled and then flared across the sky before fading.

He wrapped his arms around her, pulling her close and gazing into her eyes. "I think that was your sign. This is where you belong, here with me. From now on we run away together."

"Yes," she said nodding, smiling happily. "Yes."

"Welcome to the family. You're a Buchanan now."

HOLLINGTON HOMECOMING

Where old friends reunite…
and new passions take flight.

Book #1 by Sandra Kitt
RSVP WITH LOVE
September 2009

Book #2 by Jacquelin Thomas
TEACH ME TONIGHT
October 2009

Book #3 by Pamela Yaye
PASSION OVERTIME
November 2009

Book #4 by Adrianne Byrd
TENDER TO HIS TOUCH
December 2009

Ten Years. Eight Grads. One weekend.
The homecoming of a lifetime.

KIMANI
ROMANCE

www.kimanipress.com
www.myspace.com/kimanipress

KPHHSP

REQUEST YOUR
FREE BOOKS!

2 FREE NOVELS
PLUS 2 *FREE GIFTS!*

KIMANI
ROMANCE

Love's ultimate destination!

KRDMC

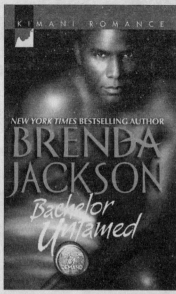